The Shining Ones

# THE SHINING ONES

## THE GUARDIANS OF LIGHT SERIES
### *BOOK TWO*

## Kasey Hill

Azoth Khem Publishing
Huntsville, AL
April 2025

# AZOTH KHEM

*For my Luxina, the starchild*

# Check out these other series by Kasey Hill

## The Guardians of Light Series
Firefly of Immortality
The Shining Ones
Firefly: The Half-Blood Angel
The Valley of the Shadow of Death: Nephilim Rising

## Dark Woods Series
Devil's Claw

## The Whispering Spirits Series
The Haunting at Foxwood Village
Dark Coven

## *Coming Soon to The Guardians of Light Series*
Firefly of Immortality II
Black Wings of Death
Firefly of Immortality: Anniel Unveiled
Alpha and Omega
Firefly of the Apocalypse

## *Coming Soon to The Guardians of Light Series Universe*

## The Guardians of Light: Darkness Falls Series
Bloodlines: Into the Shadows

The Shining Ones

# PROLOGUE: SOPHIE

I SAT ON BENDED KNEE, both in love and with my heart shattering into pieces.

In my arms, I held the light of the world. In my heart, I left the dark half of my soul abandoned and dwindling away. I substituted lust for love, and in the end, lust won. I was ashamed and broken. I don't know how many ways one's heart can be ripped from their chest and still be able to live, breathe, and function. I sat at the threshold where succumbing to darkness and resisting the light of heaven's gates was imminent. Without my other half, the reason for fighting for all these years, the prophecy seen through my own angelic eyes, I feel like an empty shell. Even with a piece of him sleeping in my arms, I was filled with hatred and bitterness. I wasn't given a choice. They chose my destiny for me. Along with the tumultuous pain also came a deepened sadness and regret at the loss of my first child. Alpha would pay for his misdeeds.

The sleeping baby stirred in my arms, and my motherly nature instantly kicked in. It was my sole duty to protect this child; this miracle granted to me by the supreme powers that be. He was the only piece I had left of the love I left behind in the darkness of the earthly realm. His name was Xavier, and he was the only light left in the dwindling ashes of the angel I once was. There was a reason I was gifted this bundle of joy and happiness. If anyone wanted to get to him, they would have to go through me.

I grinned through my chagrin at the beautiful eyes that stared up at me. He looked just like his father. His dark hair and crystal blue eyes were nothing but reminders of the man I was tethered to. I cooed as I grasped his tiny finger in my hand and rubbed small circles against the back of his palm. I had been through hellfire and brimstone. I had died and was brought back to life. I was lost, but this gift saved what small part of love I hadn't been stripped of. I had feared I couldn't go on without my love, without my Incaendiel. I had feared that I would lose myself by losing him. I feared I would pine away by losing my son to the hands of Alpha. I had reason to live now.

"Mommy will never leave you," I whispered as I kissed his forehead. "And no one will ever hurt you…"

# XAVIER

I had often watched my mother stare off into the dark void of the universe. Her eyes would always seem lifeless, and a single tear would slide down her cheek occasionally. As a younger child, I would often run to her and throw my arms around her to cheer her up. She would always look down at me, and I could see her eyes brighten just a tad. She would return the hug by picking me up and squeezing me and then set me back down where she could return back to her forlorn gaze into space.

Grandmother Lilith was the one who took my hand and showed me the infinite possibilities of who I was. Mother rarely stayed in the Summit. She was quite often with hunting parties, looking for my half-brother, Damian. Alpha took him. For what reason, only he knows, but he made sure there was a gap in my family to where we would never be happy together.

Grandmother always told me how special I was. She had never told Alpha, but when she made my parents, she made them different than all the other angels. They both possessed the powers over fire and emotions, and they were both unique. She called them twin flames. I often sat in admiration of the stories she would tell me about my father. He sounded like such a wonderful person and the bravest of all angels. She told me there was something special about me as well, but she couldn't quite put her finger on it, not just yet.

And then my dreams began.

I was three the first time I ever had a dream. Angels don't have dreams, so when I asked Grandmother about it, she laughed it off. It wasn't until I started telling her details about my dreams that she started paying attention to what I was saying. I can still remember my first dream of her…

*I awoke in a field. Most would think children would be terrified, but I was not. It was rather strange. I was… calm and at peace. As I sat up from my laying position, I heard a whimper and turned toward where the sound echoed. Just beyond the meadow of flowers was a tree, and a beautiful, shining girl sat there beneath the canopy of leaves crying. She was my age, and her hair was so red it put cardinals to shame. I walked cautiously to her so as not to frighten her anymore. I stood at the edge of the mound that the tree grew upon and waited for her to acknowledge me there.*

*She glanced up, wide-eyed and backed away from me quickly, tripping backward. I ran over to her and reached my hand out to her to help her to her feet. She was hesitant at first but smiled, taking it. An explosive bright flash illuminated the valley and sent us careening back to the ground. We set up from the ground, and the entire valley had been leveled to dust. She started to cry. I held up a finger and smiled. Grandmother taught me how to grow plants with my powers. She said I was just like my father.*

*I put my finger on the ground, and it began to glow as green grass spread all around us. The wheatgrass popped back up as well as the wildflowers in the meadows. The only thing that had stood untouched was the willow tree behind us. Everything else I restored back. When I finished, I stood back up and looked at her, smiling at me. Neither of us spoke a word to one another. We just stared as if we both were in awe of the other. I held my hand up in the air while she just watched me. Grandmother had been working with me on controlling my fire powers. I lit my hand on fire, and she was startled for a moment. She smiled at me and lifted her hand in the air. She did the same thing, lighting her hand on fire.*

*We giggled while staring at each other. She placed her hand against mine, and a small light began to shine between our palms. The flames died down as the light grew brighter, and soon, the entire valley was lit up like the sun. We gaped in awe at the colors that flowed around us. The sparkling lights danced throughout the sky. We locked our eyes and grinned at one another.*

I STARTLED awake in the Summit as Grandmother shook me. I had fallen asleep in the Garden again. I looked around at the newly sprouting flowers and foliage. A couple of the higher-ranked angels stood by her side as she stared at me both in awe and fear.

"What happened, Grandmother? What is

wrong?" I asked her.

She motioned for the others to leave us to talk. They went on their way, and she sat down beside me.

"You met someone in your dreams this time, didn't you?" she asked me.

I nodded.

"Tell me, who was it?" she asked, craning her neck.

"I don't know her name. We didn't speak to each other," I replied.

She smiled. "So, you met a girl. What was she like?" She brought her legs into a cross-legged position and leaned forward, putting her hands under her chin to listen.

"She was... beautiful," I whispered, looking off into space. "Her eyes were a marvelous green, almost like emeralds but more exquisite. Her hair was like fire, even though it doesn't compare. Her skin was like milk with drops of honey mixed. And when we touched hands, the sky exploded in swirling colors and dancing lights... she looked like Mom would have at our age, I suppose..."

I looked at Grandmother, who sat there both alarmed and serene. "What is wrong, Grandmother?"

8

"Nothing, Xavier. When you two finally talk… I would love to know her name," she replied, smiling. "Anything else you can remember about her?"

I thought for a moment. "Oh, she shines just like us," I replied.

Grandmother stopped mid-smile while it slowly faded.

"Who is she, Grandmother?" I asked.

"I… I don't know, Xavier," she replied in a distant tone, staring off down to earth. She snapped back to my face and smiled big at me. "Your mother should be returning tonight. How about we make her something special?" she asked.

"Alright," I grinned. I loved making Mother presents. However, Mother never returned that night. In fact, she didn't return for a long time.

My dreams of the girl with the red hair started happening more frequently as I grew older. We began speaking with one another and soon, I learned her name was Luxina. I went to Grandmother the moment I learned her name, just as she had asked, and she frowned.

"Xavier, there isn't a single angel in the Summit whose name is Luxina," she replied.

I grinned back. "She doesn't live here in the

Summit, Grandmother. She lives on Earth with her father," I replied.

I received the same wide-eyed stare from her that I did when I first told her about Luxina. She remained silent for a few moments as we laced flowers together in the Garden of Eden. She took me there quite often and would tell me stories about my mother and father and how in love they had been.

*"THE GARDEN WAS ALWAYS THEIRS," she replied once, with a mischievous smile. "And one day, it will be yours and your soulmate's as well."*

*"But I don't have a soulmate, Grandmother," I replied.*

*"You do. You just haven't found her in your waking world," she replied with a smile.*

NOW, as we sit here, that smile has faded into one of worry, wonder, and confusion.

"Has she ever told you her father's name?" she asked.

I shook my head in reply. "But," I started.

"But what?" Grandmother asked hurriedly.

"She says at times I look like him when I smile," I replied. "How the light twinkles around me."

Grandmother swallowed hard. "Continue with our little project, Xavier. I will return in a moment."

She returned… but she was different after her return. She no longer spent time with me in the Garden as we had always done. She began to avoid me altogether. It broke my heart. I know others in the Summit looked at me vastly differently than any of the other angel children. For one, my father was Incaendiel, the most powerful angel created. The other… well, I didn't age the way one would think angels should age. They may say they are five years old or eighteen years old or one hundred years old, but that is just by human standards. Angels age quite slowly, so for those that are only a year old, they are truthfully one thousand years old in angelic years. I was different, though. My age rapidly sped by even when compared to that of human years. I am seven years old as of today, but I look sixteen in human years. I never knew if those in the Summit feared me for who my father was… or because they didn't know WHAT I was.

But it didn't stop my dreams. In my dreams, my age didn't matter. Who I was didn't matter, for she loved me, nonetheless. I was beginning to feel tired more often and caught myself sleeping quite frequently… and she was, too… I often wondered if it was because of our unique aging because she aged as quickly as I did by angel standards. Perhaps just as humans, we hit growth spurts that tire us out.

I lay in the Garden, oftentimes dozing but never fully sleeping. I am never bothered in there, for it belongs to me. Grandmother told me so. Very few angels held the power to enter without permission. So, quite often, I slipped off into the Garden just to sleep among the wondrous plants growing in there. I closed my eyes, thinking of Luxina, smiled, and drifted off into my peaceful sleep.

*I awoke in a field. The warm sun beamed down on my face as I rose from my lying position and glanced around. Fields of summer wheat laced the earth along with wildflowers in bloom. The heavenly aroma of lavender and jasmine intoxicated me as I perused through the field. I held my hand out, brushing the tops of the flowers and wheat stalks feeling each tickle the palm of my hand. A breeze slightly blew around me, lifting the sweet notes and carrying them in the wind. A tickle of cherry blossom passed my nose, and I breathed in deeply and* closed my eyes, trying to capture the voluptuous fragrance and commit it to memory.

She was nearby.

I opened my eyes and scanned the area, trying to catch the gleam of her red hair in the beating sun's rays. A smile crawled across my face as I saw her playing peek-a-boo behind the willow tree that stood in the middle of the field. Light audible giggles drifted on the wind, tingling my ears. I loved the way she laughed.

I began my slow trek towards her as she popped in and out from behind the tree. When I was close, I crouched and sneaked up to the side of the tree she didn't peer around. As she popped her head around the tree, I crept up behind her as she looked confused out toward the field. I grabbed her by her hips, and she let out a yelp, causing me to laugh at her fright. She playfully smacked me.

"Where have you been, my sweet Firefly?" I murmured as I brushed her hair from her face.

"Battling the darkness that threatens to swallow my existence," she replied.

"It will never take you as long as you are by my side," I said, running my thumb along her lips.

"I believe you," she whispered breathlessly, staring deeply into my eyes. "I just wish we didn't solely meet in the meadow. I want to be with you in the waking world."

She took my hand in hers and kissed my knuckles lightly.

"One day, my sweet Firefly…"

I planted my lips on her forehead and rested my chin against her brow. It was moments like this I wish I could live in my dreams. Stay in this place with her. The tree we sat below… it always called to me in a whisper, an echo from years past. A familiarity. I had never stepped foot on earth, but the forlorn pull of this tree was full of love and heartache.

"Father is moving us again," she whispered. "He hasn't told me where, but there is a dread to this move that I cannot shake."

"Why do you feel dread?" I asked, running my fingers through her hair.

"I fear… I fear for our lives."

I pulled her away from my chest and gazed into her eyes. I could see the storm brewing behind them and feel her terror.

"Know this, my firefly: if anything were to happen to you, I would search the ends of your world for you and bring you back safely. Always remember my words to you. Through the mountains and over the sea, the firefly will cease to be. Over the valley and through the meadow, the firefly exists in the shadows. Fly away,

14

*firefly, until we meet again. Maybe next time, it won't be a dream that I get to hold your hand. If you were to disappear from our safe haven, and not meet as we have for years, I will come for you, do you understand? And my hand will pull you back into safety." I whispered it a bit harsher than I wanted.*

*The sun began to set in the meadow, which signaled the end of our meeting. I held her tightly, fearing it was truly our last time together, before the stars blinked her away from me. However, unlike before, when I immediately awoke as well, this time it was different. I had no idea how to will myself awake either. It always ended at twilight.*

*I watched as balls of fire emerged in the sky and plummeted to the earth, striking and exploding. The blowback from the impact hit me in barrels of wind. I watched as the mountains around the valley caught alight as they rained down on the meadow. One barreled straight for the center of the fields, and I quickly ran behind the willow tree to brace for the close impact. The wind tore around my body as the ball fire struck the heart of the field. I dug my feet into the ground and wrapped my arms around the trunk of the willow, burying my face in the bark.*

*When the wind died down and the loud earth-shaking sounds dissipated, I peeked from around the tree to*

15

*witness the devastation. Everything had been destroyed. I looked at the sky and saw a sneering face staring back at me. Its mouth opened in a huge grin, and the sounds of its evil laughter filled my ears. I covered them, but even my hands couldn't prevent the voice from piercing my senses.*

*"Oh, what a precious sight you are," it hissed. "Soon, you will be mine, for all creation is MINE! You are never safe, even in your dreams, young firefly!"*

I snapped from the dream in a panic, gasping for air. Swarms of angels surrounded me in fear. Metatron stood before me extending his hand out to help me to my feet.

"What happened? Why is everyone here?" I asked, dazed.

His eyes glanced around the Garden and back to me. I followed his eyes and saw that the same devastation to my field had happened right here in the Garden… and there was nothing but dust left.

"Fireballs rained down on the garden all around you as you screamed," Metatron replied in a barely audible whisper. "You called out for help, but no one could wake you."

I placed my hand on the ground in agony. I had destroyed my safe haven in the Summit. Not even my powers could bring it back. Or had I?

"I need to speak with Grandmother," I murmured.

Metatron stiffened at the request. "She has sworn off all visitors and requested no one to be allowed in to see her."

"I NEED to see her," I said, walking up to him. "My life… our lives are in great danger!"

"The only danger around here is you, Xavier," he retorted.

"It was Alpha!" I barked louder than I intended.

Gasps filled the empty Garden.

"Please, Metatron. She is all I must turn to. Mother…" I swallowed the lump back, forming in my throat. "Grandmother would know what it means."

"I will pass her the message, but I am afraid that is all I can do," he replied guiltily.

It was days before she would see me. Metatron came for me the day she granted my request to go before her. He led me to her throne room and left us to speak alone.

"Why do you call on me when I have asked for no visitors," she asked coolly.

"Grandmother, why have you changed in demeanor toward me?" I asked.

"I haven't changed, dear one. I have just simply been in retreat to think," she replied. "So, quickly, tell me what you need to tell me and be on your way."

"You used to spend every day with me. You used to look at me with admiration and not with the same stares I receive from everyone else here. So, beg my pardon, but you have indeed changed, Grandmother," I replied.

"Well, what did you expect!" she hissed. "You destroyed my Garden. My first creation of thriving life!"

"It was not I who destroyed the Garden," I replied.

"Oh, it was you, you, and your differentness. Your dreams seized your powers and nearly leveled the Summit!" she yelled.

"Again, it was not I. It was Alpha," I replied.

She laughed. "Do you honestly think I would believe that?"

"It is the truth. He spoke to me at the end of my dream. He told me he was coming for me!" I was outraged she wouldn't believe me.

"If I knew the tower could contain you, I would lock you away in it! You are a danger to us all, Xavier!" She stared at me without any emotion. "You are just like your father!"

"Yeah, my father was the one who saved you all! My father is the reason you get to rule from the throne you sit so 'modestly' upon, Grandmother. So, telling me I am just like him is nothing but a compliment to my ears." She pursed her lips. "If I am such a bother, I will leave."

"Good, you were starting to riddle my last nerve," she replied, rubbing her forehead.

"No one in the Summit will have to worry about me 'damaging' it or bringing them to destruction, chaos, or ruins. And if my mother ever returns, tell her she can find me with my father," I replied, turning away to leave.

"Xavier, you cannot leave!" Grandmother ordered.

"Why stay?" I asked, as I whipped around to face her. "The only person who ever loved me more than all who stood around her sits here and treats me like I am a disease! My mother loves Damian far more than she does me, or else she wouldn't have spent all my growing years chasing after him. I have no one here! They all fear me! They all hate me! They all wish I didn't exist! They all wish for me to be locked away like my mother was for millenniums!!! Including you, Grandmother. So pray, tell me, why?! Why should I stay?" I asked as tears streamed down my cheeks.

She didn't utter a word. I didn't know if she was fighting back emotions or if she truly had nothing to say.

"That is all the answer I need, Grandmother."

I left her throne room. Metatron walked nimbly behind me as I dashed for the records room.

"You are forbidden to be in here, Xavier. You know the punishment! Mother will—"

"Will what?" I asked, interrupting him. "Lock me away in the tower that won't keep me? Oh yes, she's already said she wished she could right before I told her I was leaving, so she didn't have to worry about me anymore, nor do you."

I rummaged through the files and couldn't find what I was looking for. I tore down boxes and threw scrolls aside.

"What is it you seek?" he asked apologetically.

"I need to know where my father is so I can go to him. None of you wish to keep me around, including Grandmother. Mother is never here, always off traipsing the galaxy looking for her precious son. I can't do this anymore. I don't belong here," I replied, throwing scroll after scroll on the ground.

"That isn't true," he said as he placed his hand on my shoulder. "We are just afraid of your powers. The gifts that your parents passed to you."

"Well, you don't have to fear them any longer," I replied.

My eyes landed on the Book of Life. I walked over and stared at it. It glowed golden hues and listed every creature ever born into existence and their current location.

"It is forbidden to look in that book, and you know it!" Metatron hissed.

"Well, then maybe purgatory would best suit me, right?" I asked as I flipped it open.

"Xavier, stop!" a voice hissed.

I turned around to see my mother standing there.

"What are you doing?!" she asked angrily.

"I am leaving. I am going to my father. No one wants me here nor needs me here," I replied, scanning through all the names.

"I w—"

"You!" I laughed. "You are never here! You care more about Damian than your son, who sits in pine for you every day! The son you abandoned so you could seek out the half of the family that makes your family with Lucifer whole! I haven't seen you in so long, I lost count of the days. Hell, I lost count of the months!"

I continued looking for my father's name as she stood there gaping at me.

"What? Oh, did I hurt your feelings? I am sorry, Mother. I am a rotten son. I am a terrible angel who no one here likes, including Grandmother, who wishes to lock me away in the tower that you called home for so long," I seethed.

"What?" she asked breathlessly.

"Oh, you heard me! I went to her because of my dreams and—"

"You have dreams?" she asked.

"Well, if you were around longer than just a few moments in time, you would know this, but yes, Mother, I have dreams," I replied in disdain. "I am treated like a leper here. I hate it here!! I hate the stares! The whispers! The laughter behind my back! I hate that Grandmother, the one person who I thought loved me, now wishes I never existed. I never did anything! Do you all think I want to be different? Do you all think I want unique gifts? I am a pariah! The laughingstock of the Summit!"

Mother and Metatron both stood quietly as I finished searching the book for his name.

"Why isn't he in here?!" I yelled as I threw the book to the floor and kicked it away.

I slid to the ground in tears. Mother walked over to me and sat down beside me. She placed her hand on my shoulder, and I yelled, "Don't touch me!"

"No one can find your father, Xavier. He has powers that hide him from everyone," she stated softly.

I sobbed into my hands. "Why doesn't anyone want me?"

"I want you!" she cried.

"No, you just want something that reminds you of him. You don't want me. You want a memory," I replied, wiping my nose on my sleeve.

She looked like someone punched her in the gut.

"You feel that?" I asked. "Because that is what it feels like to be me every day, knowing that truth. Knowing that I am not what is important."

I stood from my seated position and headed for the door when Metatron stepped in front of me.

"Go ahead," I said. "Lock me away. I don't care. I won't escape. Why would I?"

Metatron threw his arms around me and squeezed me into his chest. "I wasn't able to keep my promise to your mother about Damian, but I will never leave your side, Xavier. That is a promise I will always keep, even if it is to myself."

"It doesn't matter," I replied. "Alpha will find me and take me just as he promised."

He pulled away from me with his hands firmly planted on my shoulders.

"What?" he asked.

"It's why I requested to speak to Grandmother. But she doesn't care either way. She would be glad to be rid of me even if it was to him," I replied.

"What do you mean?" Mother asked, standing to her feet.

She began to glow red as her anger bubbled.

"In my dream, Alpha was the one who rained down the fireballs and told me he would find me because I was his creation. He finds all his creations," I replied.

She turned to Metatron. "You promised him just now, and you *will* promise me that *nothing* and *no one* will *ever* take him! Do you understand me?!" she hissed.

"Yes, Sophie," he replied. "You have my word."

"You failed me once, Brother. Do not fail me again!" she said as she hastily walked off.

"Where are you going?" he asked.

"To see, Mother. She has some explaining to do!" she yelled as she erupted in flames.

"I need to make sure she doesn't burn down the Summit. Will you be okay for a few moments alone? Promise not to run away?" he asked.

I nodded. He walked me from the room and took off after Mother. I walked through the center of the Summit as all eyes trained on me. I could hear the whispers. I could feel the fear.

"There you are!" I heard a familiar voice yell out. "Where you been, buddy?" Lucifer asked as he threw his arm around me.

I never liked Lucifer. Had it not been for him, my family wouldn't be in the shambles it is in right now.

"Around," I murmured.

"Where you off to?" he asked.

"The Garden," I replied, as I shrugged his arm from around my neck. "And no, you do not have my permission to come along."

"Fair enough," he replied.

I walked numbly to the Garden and sank to my knees, crying. It was nothing but burned rubble. Every part of my soul cried out as I sat there on my knees in agony. My gut had been true. Grandmother did hate me, and I haven't the slightest idea as to why. I leaned forward and put my forehead to the ground as I sobbed out all the pain: the pain of not having a mother, the pain of not having my father, the pain of being lonely. Luxina popped into my head, and I cried even harder. Would I ever see her again since our meeting place had been destroyed? Would I ever hold her hand again? Swipe the hair from her face? Kiss her forehead?

I pounded the ground I lay upon and felt the earthquake beneath the blow. I rolled over to my back and peered up at the twinkling stars that hovered above my precious abode. I just want to be loved. Is that so much to ask for? I know... I know I have darkness in me, just like my father. And everyone is terrified of that darkness, but they don't make the darkness any better than what it is. Everyone, that is, besides Luxina. She is the light of my world, the flashlight in the dark, the lighthouse in my storm. I no longer fear my darkness whenever I am with her, for her light outshines it.

I felt something tickle my hand and looked over at it while wiping the tears from my eyes with my other hand. A firefly had landed on my hand. I stared at it as it sat there with me in my misery and grief. It was beautiful. I looked past the firefly, and my eyes widened. There was green grass beneath my hand. I carefully sat up so as not to disturb the creature that graced me with its presence and looked around the Garden. It twinkled as lights danced around, touching everything that had been destroyed and healing it. Every blackened, charred spot returned to its luscious green state. The flowers budded and bloomed. The trees sprouted their leaves. The animals returned to graze. I stared in astonishment at the renewed Garden.

"You are just like him, you know?"

I looked up to see my mother standing there.

"Your father," she started, with a smile, "your father was remarkable. Anything destroyed, he could return to its original state of being. Especially when he cried out his pain."

The firefly flew from my finger and circled her, landing on her outstretched hand. She nuzzled the creature, and it took off into the breeze. She walked over to me and sat down beside me, admiring the Garden.

"This was my favorite place," she said, gazing around. "Mother gave it to me and your father a long time ago."

I sat there silently, just looking around at the still-growing Garden.

"Xavier," she began, "you are loved, my son. I love you more than the stars, more than the moon, more than myself even. You were the only thing that kept me going when we returned to the Summit, and your father stayed behind. I needed you. I wanted you more than anything in the world."

I sat there and listened as she cooed at me, running her fingers through my hair.

"You look so much like him," she said, smiling. "Some days, I stop myself from calling you by his name. And you two brood the same way. I always wished I could reach inside his heart so he could feel and know how much I loved him. I wish the same for you."

"Then, stay with me," I said. "Stay with me this time instead of leaving with the rest of them. I need you, Mother. I need you here with me!"

Her eyes dropped from mine.

"I know it is selfish of me to say, but you have a son here that needs you. You have a son here that has no one left to love him. If you love me, you will stay with me!" I begged.

I watched a tear slide down her cheek.

"It's not that easy, Xavier," she whispered.

"It is, Mother. It is that easy!" I replied harshly. "Let Lucifer go alone this time! For once, pay attention to your child begging for your love."

"I can't," she replied.

I nodded, holding back the welling emotions.

"I'm sorry for you, then," I replied.

"Why?" she asked, confused.

"Because I won't be here waiting for you next time. I won't be like Father. I won't wait around hoping and wishing and wanting for you to realize that I am important."

I could see the knife stab her in the heart with that last statement.

"Please, just let me be," I stated.

I stood up and walked further into the Garden. I sat there until the sun filled the Garden, and then, I sat there longer.

"It isn't fair of you to ask her to stay."

"It isn't fair of her not to stay," I replied. "It isn't fair that she treats me the same way she did Father."

Grandmother sat down beside me and watched as the sun rose.

"I see you fixed the Garden," she said.

"It appears as though I did," I replied.

I refused to look at her. Everything I had ever held on to so tightly I let go of when Mother left the Garden.

"Your dark cloud is circling you today," she said.

"And so it is," I replied unfeelingly.

"Xavier, I—"

"Oh, what? You're sorry?" I asked, cutting her off. "It's a bit late for that, oh, Dark One."

"I didn't mean what I said to you yesterday," she replied.

"Oh, I'm sure you didn't. But don't worry, Grandmother. I don't have a hit list with names, so you are safe from my reign of terror everyone thinks of," I spat.

"I broke you, but I can fix it," she began.

"No one can fix this now," I replied. "I received all the answers I needed yesterday. So, just let me sit here and allow this wound in my chest to fester."

"Xavier, you are letting the dark consu—"

"Consume me? The darkness is me, just like Father. All that you all ever cared about was getting back here, whether it meant he was to be sacrificed or not. Of all people, YOU KNEW he wasn't coming back. But you let everyone believe he was."

She was quiet for a moment.

"Your mother asked me what I thought she should do. If she should stay, or if she should go and continue to look for Damian," she stated.

"And what did you say?" I asked, looking at her.

"I told her she should stay," she replied.

"Did she?" I asked.

She shook her head. "No, she left this morning with the rest of them."

I nodded my head and held back the tears.

"It's always nice to feel second best in life," I said, holding back the tears threatening to spill.

"I am here for you," Grandmother cooed.

"Are you? Or are you going to lock yourself away again? Belittle me when I come to you about my dreams?" I hissed.

"I am sorry. I was upset about the Garden being destroyed," she replied.

"Yeah, and wouldn't even acknowledge the fact that I didn't do it. Everything is always my fault!" I fumed.

"That was unfair of me, I agree. I am sorry about that. I should not have acted the way I did to you or said the things I did to you," she replied.

"Oh, you mean like locking me away in the tower?" I asked.

"I don't know why I said those things," she replied, thinking deeply. "I wasn't myself."

"Alpha is coming," I said flatly. "He is coming for me. He knows about me. No one could stop him from taking Damian, so no one can stop him from taking me."

"He will not take you!" she seethed. "You are not HIS! You are MINE! He will NOT have you!"

"He destroyed the meadow Luxina and I would meet in," I stated. "The fireballs were in the meadow."

"What else happened in the dream?" she asked.

"The normal part. We met and spent time together. She told me her father was moving them again, but she had a bad feeling about it this time," I replied.

"And you said she ages just like you, right? That you two have aged and look the same age?" she asked.

"Yes," I replied. "We both look like we are sixteen even though we are only seven years old."

"When did the dream change this time?" she asked.

"Twilight approached the field, and normally, we just wake up after saying goodbye. She disappeared, but I didn't wake up this time. Instead, huge balls of fire plummeted down and burned everything. When the last one fell, and the dust settled, there was a face in the stars laughing at me. That's when he said what I told you before," I replied.

"Do you know if he knows about Luxina?" she asked, a bit alarmed.

"I don't know. Who knows how long he had been spying on us," I replied.

Metatron appeared at the doorway of the Garden.

"Excuse me for a moment," she said.

I watched as she whispered to him, and he nodded and bowed to her, leaving the doorway. He returned moments later, and I read his lips as he said, "He hasn't moved yet."

She smiled and thanked him as he left the Garden. She walked back over to me and resumed her seated position. I eyed her, wanting her to break her silence, but she didn't.

"You know a secret, don't you?" I asked.

She glanced over at me, worry streaking her brow.

"I can't tell you, Xavier. I can't even tell your mother what I know," she replied.

"Well, what do you know?" I asked.

She sighed heavily. "One day… just not today."

I nodded my head. "Okay," I replied quietly. I debated back and forth with myself for what seemed like an eon before I spoke again. "Grandmother?"

"Yes, child?" she replied.

"I want to see my father. Please take me to see him," I asked, my voice trembling.

"Xavier, I know nothing about your father since we left the Glade. I don't know if…" she began.

"If what?" I asked.

"I don't know if he has moved on from your mother and found someone to start a family with again," she replied.

"He doesn't know about me," I said. "He deserves to know about me."

She looked at me long, hard, and deep. She breathed deeply and exhaled. "Alright. I will take you to him. *But* he is not to see you!" she hissed.

"Yes, ma'am," I replied, grinning.

She took my hand in hers, and before I knew it, we were on earth. I didn't know where we were, but we were here. She motioned for me to be quiet as we watched a young man walk down the back alley from a diner. He carried two platters of food in Styrofoam boxes. *So, he has moved on to another family*, I thought solemnly.

He turned around quickly, and Grandmother cloaked us. I watched him as he stared in our direction, squinting. He felt our presence. He began to jog over to a car and hopped into the driver's seat. He was gone in a flash. Grandmother blinked us to his house, as he pulled into the drive. He ran inside and later emerged with a young redheaded girl. My heart quickened as I struggled to see her face. That hair... her hair was exactly the same as Luxina's hair. The car lights were turned off, so I couldn't see her face. He ran inside and grabbed a few bags, throwing them into the backseat and sped off.

"Well, we spooked him," she said. "Was that enough to satisfy your need?" she asked.

"The girl with him... her hair... she looks just like Luxina from behind," I murmured, walking to the car speeding off.

33

"Xavier, it is best to leave things alone," Grandmother warned.

"I can't," I whispered, as I sped off toward the car.

I followed them for miles as they passed from state to state. I had to know for sure. I had to know if it was her. It would make sense, so much sense. Mother and Father were created as twin souls. Luxina and I could be an exact replica of them! It was early dawn when they reached their destination. He led her inside a quaint tiny home, and I stood outside watching, cloaked. I had to see her face, just one moment, to know it was her.

"Xavier!" Grandmother hissed, as she spun me around. "We must return. We have been gone for far too long, and the longer we are here, the more dangerous it is for us!"

I turned to the house and watched as my father exited the front door. I swear it was as if he were staring directly at me.

"Can he see me?" I whispered.

"No, nor can he hear us. I have powers of my own, you know?" she replied curtly. "We must go. You saw him. You must not interfere with his new life."

I nodded. "Okay, Grandmother."

Just as she blinked us away and back to the Summit, the front door opened, and the redheaded girl stepped out into the sunlight. Her hair was covering her face and just as she went to brush it out of her way with her hand, we were back in the Summit.

Grandmother grabbed me by my shoulders and shook me. "You must NEVER do that again!" She stared at me. "Do you realize the danger you are in while on earth? Alpha…" She stopped.

"I know, and I am sorry, Grandmother. My mind got away from me," I replied, ashamed. "I promise to never do it again if you ever take me back."

"We don't even know if this Luxina person is in league with Alpha. She could be another one of his…"

"Another one of his what?" I asked.

Grandmother stared past me, and my eyes followed her gaze. It was Mother.

"Sophie, what are you doing back so soon?" she asked. "Did you find him?!"

Mother glanced back and forth between Grandmother and me.

"No," she sighed. "But I have come to realize," she began, staring me in the eyes, "that I have spent far too long on this mission and not enough time with my son, who is right here."

I smirked back at her. "Oh really? So, just like that, you think it is more important to be here with me and not hunting for your precious Damian?"

"Xavier, I know I am not perfect. I have never claimed to be. I never thought it would take this long to find Damian. But I have recognized what a lost cause it is and ask for your forgiveness," Sophie replied.

I shook my head violently. "No, no, no!" I screamed. "You don't just get to walk back into my life and act as if nothing ever happened. You don't get to act like my mother when you haven't been one for the last seven years!"

"Xavier," Grandmother cooed, interrupting. "Give it a chance. You mi—"

I quickly intercepted her sentence and cut her off. "I might what? I might find that I have a lot in common with my mother? I might find that she cares more for me than I realize? No, the only person who ever gave a morsel of love to me was you and even you abandoned me!"

"I did it to protect—"

"Protect me? Protect yourself? Who are you protecting now, Grandmother? You would all rather Damian was here as opposed to me! The precious prodigal son that was stolen away from my whore of a mother," I spat.

"That's not fair!" Sophie yelled, with tears welling in the brims of her eyes. "I love you no more nor less than your older brother! I just want my son back!! Why is that hard for you to understand?!"

"Because I am standing right here! I have always been standing right here! Waiting for you to return. Waiting for you to acknowledge me for more than a mere moment before leaving me to return to your hunt! I wanted a mother that loved me. I wanted a mother that wanted me! But I only got one that wanted what she didn't have and spent an eternity looking for it!" I started to walk away but stopped. "Don't give up looking for your precious Damian now, Mother. You're going to need a son after today because I no longer see you as my mother. You were just the woman who spawned me. I have no family."

"Xavier!" Sophie called out as I walked away.

"Let him be," Grandmother replied quietly as I entered the Garden.

Everything I walked past instantly died on spot. My emotions were rampant and killing the Garden once more.

"You know, you're a selfish brat!" a voice seethed in the distance.

"I did not grant you permission to enter, Lucifer. So please, leave," I replied through gritted teeth.

"You don't scare me, little boy," Lucifer said, spinning me around by my shoulder.

I landed a punch square in his jaw, and his eyes blazed at me. He reared back to sock me when I lost control of any hold I had on my power. He grabbed at his throat as the earth blackened beneath his feet. He coughed and wheezed and spat dust in the air from his lungs as they slowly filled with burning decay as he began to incinerate and die from the inside out.

"Xavier! No!" Sophie called out as she ran to me.

I was too far gone. I turned my gaze to her, and she stopped in her tracks, gasping. However, I am her child for a reason, and my powers came to be from her and my father. She pounded her fist onto the ground, and a line of fire blazed in a path straight to me, encircling me in a hot, fiery crater. I was too distracted by the heat to hold my power over them any longer than I had. They both gasped as the air hit their lungs and spat and sputtered until the oxygen normalized in their breath.

"We have to lock him away as Mother suggested," Lucifer bellowed. "His powers are advancing and in such a dark way!"

"No! I refuse to let my son suffer the way I did for centuries. Anyone who tries will have to answer to me!" Sophie seethed. "Do you want to test me as well, Lucifer?" Her eyes lit with fire as she stood her ground in between Lucifer and me. She glanced back at me as her hands blazed and returned her glare to him.

"You chose this wretched waste of space over finding Damian! Just like you chose his father over me repeatedly. I believe it is time you learned a lesson of your own," he smirked and snapped his fingers.

Angels surrounded Sophie at the command of Lucifer. However, they weren't the everyday angels that lived at the Summit. These were the wayward angels that had turned dark, called The Forsaken. Flames engulfed Sophie as her powers bloomed with fury.

"Do it now!" Lucifer hissed.

From nowhere, a weighted net fell over top of her. She hit the ground with her fire snuffing out. She was completely powerless. She struggled under the net, but it was futile. She was trapped.

"What is that?!" I yelled, running to her aid.

Lucifer snagged me and held me with one of his hands as I struggled to free myself.

"It's a net made from unicorn hair. The only thing strong enough to bind angelic powers," Lucifer sneered.

"Take her to the tower and mark the door so no one can enter. We can't have mother dearie chasing after us," Lucifer laughed.

Two of the Forsaken picked up Sophie and wrapped her in the net so she couldn't escape. Lucifer pushed me off to two others standing there, and they held me still.

"Oh, and Beelzebub, be careful with her, would you?" Lucifer smirked. "We still need her for our plan."

"No problem, Brother," Beelzebub replied.

"One of you needs to grab Lilith as well," Lucifer barked at the rest of the Forsaken standing there.

"Sir, she fled the Summit already," one replied.

"We will hunt for her later, then," he hissed in anger. "As for you," he said, motioning to me with his pointer finger. "Alpha is going to have a field day with you. There won't be any need to experiment on you. You are already dark, just like your father."

I struggled against the two Forsaken holding me back. When they wouldn't let go, I seared their hands with my powers, and they howled in pain, letting me slip free. Freedom was short-lived, however. Lucifer scooped me up in some sort of bag I couldn't escape from.

"No use in trying, kiddo," Lucifer snorted. "It's designed to render you powerless."

"What do you want with me? Why are you handing me over to Alpha? I have never done anything to you!" I asked, scratching at the cloth on the inside of the bag. He jostled me as he walked.

"You should already know. Alpha has my son, Damian. Alpha wants you. It's a fair and even trade to me. Why settle for a half-blood angel when he can have you? He wants you more than Damian."

"Why does he want me so bad?" I demanded.

"Damian only has half of your power. He only has your mother as his parent. You are Incaendiel's and Sophie's child. He is going to be pleased with the efforts we have concocted." Lucifer stopped. "We have one more stop after sending him to Alpha. We must pay Incaendiel a little visit. Alpha says that he has another just like Xavier with him, but it is unclear as to whose spawn she is," he dictated to those around him. "She is to be unharmed and delivered in a loving condition. Her name is Luxina."

*Luxina! No! Why does Incaendiel have Luxina?* I couldn't believe my ears. My father was with Luxina. *But they have no clue who she is, which means Alpha doesn't either.*

"Grandmother was wrong," I whispered.

"What are you mumbling?" Lucifer asked, irritated.

Before I could answer, someone else spoke. "Do you have Xavier?" a younger voice asked.

"He is bagged and tagged," Lucifer replied.

"Excellent. Alpha will be pleased with this news," the voice replied.

"It won't be long, son," Lucifer said.

*Son?!*

"Do not call me that! You don't deserve nor have the right to refer to me as your son. Alpha is my father," he replied.

*DAMIAN!*

# Firefly: The Half-Blood Angel

## Introduction

# XAVIER AND DAMIAN MEET

"LET ME GO! I want to see him!" I yelled, struggling inside the bag.

"Shut up!" he yelled back at me. "You will come to find my terms more pleasing than that of which Alpha has planned for you. At least when I trade these two lab rats for your freedom, he won't be experimenting on you any longer," Lucifer retorted to Damian. "Your brother—"

"Don't you dare talk about my brother as if he is yours! You hate him. You have freely admitted your loathing of him, of which I am sure the feeling is mutual. However, you will not speak ill of him in my presence. He is innocent of your hatred. He is my—"

"Lucifer. Damian. Welcome back!"

"Hello, Father," Lucifer replied, dropping me to the ground still wrapped up in the bag.

*Where the hell are we?* I thought to myself. *We traveled for such a brief time to get somewhere.*

"Now, let's see what goodies you have brought me," he said, opening the bag.

I stood up and faced my nightmare. There he was, the voice and face of my every nightmarish dream.

"Alpha," I hissed.

"Hello, young Xavier. It is nice to finally meet you," he replied, with a sly grin. "I have been, shall we say, watching you in your dreams for years."

I didn't say a word.

"That beautiful, young, red-haired beauty of yours... do you know who she really is?" he asked.

"I'm not telling you anything," I seethed.

"Xavier, I am God. I know everything. There is nothing you know that I don't already," he said. "However, there are things I know that you do not. Like for instance, do you know why you have special powers? I do..."

* * *

I AWOKE TO DARKNESS. I went to move, but my arms were shackled to the wall. *What is this?* I tried to break them, but they were indestructible. I remembered what Lucifer had said about the net and grimaced. I was trapped here. The light flipped on, and my eyes blurred, trying to adjust. I heard footsteps and looked up at a silhouette standing before me.

My eyes began to clear. Before me stood a red, curly-haired teenager with freckles. He looked just like me except not. I looked around him at two of the men standing behind him. I recognized them immediately as part of the troop that kidnapped me.

"Do you know who I am?" he asked.

The voice.

"Damian," I replied.

"So, you were paying attention while in the bag," he mused.

"Help me!" I pleaded. "Help me escape, brother!"

"Now, why would I do that? Soon, our sister will be here, and we will be one happy family!" he laughed.

"Our sister?" I asked, confused.

"In due time, Brother, in due time, you will learn. But for now, we have some tests to run on you."

"Tests?" I asked, shaking my head, trying to understand. "What do you mean tests?"

"Alpha has a plan for us all," Damian replied, pacing in front of me. "We will be the elite, the strongest angels in the heavens. Far stronger than our parents, be they Lucifer or Incaendiel." He stopped pacing and bent down in front of me. "This is going to hurt just a bit."

He jabbed a needle into my neck and pushed the plunger, and my skin began to crawl with fire. My blood boiled, and I howled in pain.

"What is this!!!" I screamed in agony.

"It's what Alpha likes to call Heavenly Hellfire. The old bloke doesn't understand the meaning behind the name, but that's a later discussion with him," Damian replied.

My body began to convulse, and I hit the ground, foaming at the mouth.

"It's killing me," I strangled out.

"No brother... that is where you are wrong!" Damian laughed maniacally. "It's making you stronger. It's making you like me." His eyes grew black and then went back to their original color.

"What are you?" I hissed.

Pain rippled through my body, and I screamed. It felt like pure fire ran through my blood.

"I am something no one can ever be!" he said defiantly. "But we can be this together! We can hold the power over the angels and start our own allegiance where they bow to our feet. Wouldn't you love that? Wouldn't you love for people to look at you with respect instead of disgust just because you are different from them? This is our escape."

"What would you know about being mocked," I asked, rolling over in my own vomit.

"You think they took kindly to me in the Summit? No, far from it, Brother. They treated me like a leper. I had powers they didn't understand. But Alpha, he loved me, nonetheless. I went through what you are now. It only burns the first few times. By the fourth treatment, you will be strong as an ox!"

"I don't want to be anything like you! You're a monster!" I screamed.

"Is that any way to talk to your older brother, Xavier? I saved you!" he yelled. "I saved you from your own personal hell. We heard about your dreams. We heard how all the angels were terrified of you and wanted nothing to do with you! Here," he said, turning in a circle, "it's like you are Alpha himself."

He smiled a twisted smile.

"I don't want to be like Alpha," I choked out as I vomited more foam.

He knelt in front of me again. "You will be thinking differently soon."

He stood back up and barked an order. "Unchain his one arm and give him a cot to sleep on. That's no way to treat family, especially one so highly magical."

The two Forsaken didn't budge.

"Now!" Damian bellowed.

"He may present a threat unchained," one of them replied.

"Trust me, he won't have the strength to fight back."

He left the room, and the two Forsaken walked over to me. I tried to move away, but Damian was right. I didn't have the strength to fight back.

"If Lilith finds out what is happening here, she will have all our heads on a platter," one of them seethed.

"She can't do anything to us. Besides, why would she care? She hasn't cared for how long now over Damian?" the other retorted.

"This is HER special angel. Everyone in the Summit knows how fond she is of him. She was the one who raised him. She will kill us all!" the one replied.

"Just do your job. Father will see to it that Lilith does nothing to anyone who is in on his plans. I trust Alpha, as should you. If he knew you were doubting his plans, he would skin you alive! So, hush!"

"What are his plans," I murmured.

"In due time, young one. I know you are going through pain, but it will be over soon," he replied.

I blacked out.

When I came to, Damian was standing over me.

"Good morning, Brother. Still in pain?" he asked.

The burning was mild now.

I shook my head.

"Excellent," he said as he plunged another needle into my neck.

The liquid coursed through my veins, but he was right. It didn't hurt nearly as badly as before.

"See, that's not so bad. If you can promise not to run away, I will unchain your other arm," Damian said, smiling. "I would like to properly hug my flesh and blood."

I nodded.

Two new men walked over and unchained my arm left chained to the wall. I rubbed my wrist where the shackles had been. Damian walked over to me and stood before me. Rage tore through me, and I grabbed him and twisted his arm behind his back. I grabbed a short blade sword from the table and held it to his neck.

"Let me go, and I will let him go," I stated.

"We can't do that," the two said as they walked to him.

I let go of his arm and kicked him into the two Forsaken. I picked up another blade and stood in a fighting stance. Metatron and Michael taught me sword fighting and battle techniques.

Damian composed himself.

"You want to play, is it?" he asked.

He picked up a sword and twisted it around in his hand. "Let's play."

I ran toward him, and we began to dance around in a circle. He would thrust at me, and I would block every advance. I did a roundabout kick and caught him square in the jaw. He wiped the blood from his lips, and his eyes turned black.

"Wrong move, Brother," he replied menacingly.

He tore through the room, swiping the sword through the air like a fan. I blocked each advancing strike until he knocked one of the blades from my hand. I used the other to parry the attacks until it was flung from my hands. He cornered me with the blade pointed into my chest.

"I could end you now, but Alpha wouldn't be happy!" he sneered. "I wanted us to be a family, but it seems you can't do that. Chain him back up!" he commanded. "And when does our sister get here?!" he demanded.

"Soon, Lucifer is on his way with her now," they replied.

"Give him another injection. Maybe he will pass out from a double dose. We wouldn't want him poisoning her mind. We need her to be a fresh, clean slate." He tossed the sword down.

They shackled me back to the wall. I winced as the needle hit my neck, and they pushed the fluids through with the plunger. I glared at them. There was no pain. Either I had become immune, or it had already fused with my blood. I didn't know yet."

Damian walked over to me. "This was fun, Brother. Maybe another time we can finish what we started."

I spit in his face. He wiped it off and walked over to the door. "Spend your days in the dark in here. That's all you are. A ball of darkness, just like your pathetic father," he said as he flipped the light out.

I hated the dark.

# DAMIAN

I WAS A CHILD BORN OF LIGHT and raised in darkness. I have known but one father, the All-Father, and he has raised me in accordance with his laws. My real father, a deceptive fiend, joined ranks against the only person who has ever shown me gnosis in its purest form. My mother, a whore monger, chose darkness over her livelihood in the Summit. The All-Father, Alpha, was my god and my savior,

I was pushed into training as soon as I could walk. The war among angels was imminent, and I was to be prepared to face off if necessary. If this meant killing my own parents, then so be it. They were of no use to me. They had joined the army of the Dark Mother, Lilith. She was a twisted snake that chose to fall, that chose to disobey the All-Father, her husband. She was a poison to humanity that needed to be eradicated, along with all the angels who chose to leave with her. They were the epitome of evil and disobedience.

Alpha had chosen me to be his right hand, his leverage in the holy war. I spent every day training with the elite in the Summit. Michael and Metatron taught me sword and combat fighting. My chosen weapon had been the long sword.

Ever since I was old enough to make memories, I could remember everyone in the Summit bending over backward to help me. I was the prodigal child, the spawn of Sophie and Lucifer, two of the most powerfully seated angels in the Summit. That was until I began to develop powers. They were unlike my mother's powers. Where she could set things ablaze, I could freeze things in their place. Solid blocks of ice would spring forth whenever I was emotional. Blizzards would pop up whenever I was angry. Everything would freeze over when I was sad. Everything means exactly that, everything. Even the angels within a distance of me were affected and turned into blocks of ice.

My main trigger? My mother. I wanted to be with her, but Alpha told me I was too special to meddle in the affairs going on in the mortal world. Truthfully, he didn't want me kidnapped and warped by the fallen angels, including my mother. I was too special to be warped. Alpha had a plan for me. He said my parents wouldn't understand the potential I was faced with. I was given a divine gift from the cosmos that held power even he didn't possess. They would be jealous of me. I believe he was right, too.

However, when I think about my formidable years, I am the one jealous. All I ever knew was training and battle tactics. I didn't know love. I didn't know empathy or sympathy. Alpha treated me like a soldier, not a son. And then, my mother had a child with Incaendiel. Of course, I never got to meet him. Alpha whisked me away from the fallen angels returning to the Summit, so my pure angelic nature wouldn't be tainted by their darkness. I still envy my brother, though. He was able to grow up with our mother.

I wanted everything he had. He had my home, the Summit. He had my mother, Sophie. He had Grandmother Lilith. He had it all while I was left with Alpha. I was never allowed to call him Grandfather. I was never allowed to call him Father. I was to only address him as Alpha. He hid me from the world, depriving me of any social interaction I could succumb to... and then experimented on me.

I no longer loved him. I no longer respected him. But I needed his attention and approval. I craved it. It was the only attention I ever received. When the injections began, it wasn't long after Mother had gone to Earth. I was growing unusually fast, and he wanted to test my blood against other strains of blood to see how compatible they were. He wanted to make a legion of angels just like me. Except, they really wouldn't be angels. They would be more like angel spawns that went horribly wrong.

My brother and I had one thing in common, though. We both want to get rid of Alpha. I had to keep the façade up long enough to where I could divulge my plan to Xavier about bringing down Alpha before we brought Luxina in here. However, Lucifer is thwarting my efforts, and it will only be a matter of time before she is here as well. If Alpha found out that I had been a traitor in his midst, he would dispatch me himself.

I watched my brother in stealth as he sat chained to the wall. It was fun being able to take him on in battle. He was a fighter. He proved himself to me, and I knew when the time would come, he would help me take down Alpha. I just had to keep up this façade long enough to be able to crumble Alpha to his knees. There was no doubt in the world that he cared nothing for me. I was a weapon, a disposable tool for him to pick up and play with. When the time would come for either Luxina or Xavier to surpass me in strength and agility, I am most definitely sure that he will kill me. So, I fake it as much as I can fathom. I fake the evil. I fake the strength. I don't need additional strength. I received all I needed when I was made from my mother. The only thing these stupid injections did was turn me darker, cynical, and mostly apathetic about everything.

I was much more like Xavier than he realized. I spent my life wanting things I could never have as well. Most likely, Luxina is the same way. We all come from a broken family that had no one to blame but Alpha himself. So, we must take him down at all costs.

"Damian," Lucifer called out, as he walked down the corridor to where I stood watching Xavier. "Ready to go, bud?" he asked.

"I am not nor have ever been your *bud*. Got that, Lucy?" I replied, brushing past him.

"What is your problem with me, boy?" he bellowed.

I stopped in my tracks and cracked my neck. I balled my hands into fists and whipped around to face him.

"Boy?" I asked coldly.

"Yea, *boy*," he reiterated. "You think you're a man, but you're not. You think you are Alpha's prodigal son, but you're not. You're *my* son, *my* flesh and blood. You *will* show me respect."

I squeezed my closed fists even tighter, and they cracked under the pressure.

"Or what?" I asked, glaring at him with all the hate I could fathom.

"Or I will have to teach you a lesson. I will teach you a lesson, and when I am done… I will teach that same lesson to your pathetic excuse of a brother," he replied, jabbing his finger into my collarbone.

"Big mistake," I replied, as I looked at his finger and back up to his face.

In one short, fluid movement, I had him pinned against the wall with his arm pulled up and twisted behind his back.

"Don't you *ever* threaten *me* or my family again, do you understand?" I whispered heatedly in his ear. "I will have no problem killing you and watching you die a slow and painful death."

I released my grip on him and turned to walk away. Two guards stood at the end of the hall, waiting for my signal. Lucifer rubbed his wrist and stretched out his arm as they smirked at him.

"Let's go get my sister," I stated, walking through the exit.

# The Valley of the Shadow of Death: Nephilim Rising

## Introduction

# INCAENDIEL

# PROLOGUE

I LOOK INTO THE EYES of my child, my daughter, and the world crumbles around me. A piece of myself had been momentarily lost to the light where I could not walk, where I could no longer go. A piece  that was my light, the only light that I had left in this darkness. I had  to release it; I had to let it go where it needed to go for survival. The light is fragile within chaos. The chaos of darkness would have consumed it, consumed her. She would have become one of the fallen that walk these lands full of discontent and hatred for all things living or immortal. Humanity had been spoon-fed a word for these fallen ones, the fallen angels, my brothers. Alpha had dripped into humanity evil lies, calling my forlorn brothers demons and monsters.

I fought the darkness as long as I could. I had to fight it. It was the only way to save my brothers, my fellow fallen ones. It was a battle that I hadn't won from the start. Darkness lived within me before I fell. There was no consumption once my light left during the plummet to Earth. It existed as an equal to her light, a natural harmonic balance. Our Yin and Yang energies complemented each other. When I took the plunge from the Summit, I never imagined the plan we had created would fall through. Yes, our plan was to return those who had fallen back to the Summit and return their light. She would have never guessed that my fall would have left me desolate and defeated. My light would never return. The darkness won what rightfully belonged to it, my soul.

It surprised me to find this hidden piece of light left behind. The light never belonged in the darkness, and soon, I feared the pit of doom would swallow it. However, this time, I couldn't give it up as easily as I did last time. Granted, it wasn't easy to offer up the light of my life, the love of my life, the other half of my soul to another angel to care for, but she had a family. It wasn't fair of me to take her away from the one thing she had always craved with me. I let her go. This time wouldn't be so easy. I held within my arms a truth that I couldn't just hand over to anybody, not without a fight. I would fight to keep this existence of hers and mine safe and out of harm's way. I would fight to the death anyone who would try to harm my light, my Luxina.

I flew from the mountaintop, holding her carefully in my arms. Her tiny wings would never be able to catch her if she were to fall from my arms. I landed on the ground at the entrance of my home. It was new and old all at the same time. I had lived here for millions of years, but now I would live there alone. Well, not exactly alone, for I would have her at my side still. This little child will be the only thing that gets me through the hard years for me ahead. I walked through the entrance to the Glade and made my way down the spiraled staircase. It was so empty, so abandoned. Thousands of fallen angels once resided in this home with our Mother. Now, it was just Luxina and me.

She looked so much like her mother it was uncanny. It's almost as if the cosmos left a piece of her with me that would stay with me forever. A piece of her I could keep free from guilt and not have to give up. I carried her to the room her mother stayed in most often and laid her on the bed. She cooed her baby talk, and I couldn't help but let a happy tear fall from my eyes. I curled up on the bed beside her, letting her grab my finger and pull it to her mouth. At that exact moment, I felt as if I had everything that I would ever need, even if the other half of my soul was gone. This little girl was all that I would ever need.

Her little mouth opened wide, stifling a yawn, and her eyelids drifted heavily shut. I wrapped my wing around the two of us to cover her and keep her cozy. She drifted off to sleep, and I lay there watching her sleep in my arms. The picture of perfection wrapped tightly in my protective arms. I would never let anything, or anyone harm her. To hurt her would mean death, and I would see to it that they suffered tremendously. I closed my eyes, and her mother's face haunted my mind. Our last embrace, our last kiss, so much love, and so much loss. I opened my eyes back up. I doubt I will ever sleep again, not without her by my side, not without my Sophie.

# CHAPTER 1

"DAD, DO I REALLY have to start a new school this year? I'm old enough to where they can't tell anything." Luxina sat in the car as I walked around and opened her door. "Please! I liked my old school. That's where my friends are!"

I sighed and shook my head.

"You know we can't risk staying in one place for too long. People get suspicious of not only you but of me as well." I stood there patiently waiting for her to unbuckle her seatbelt and get out of the car.

"You're paranoid! Ugh!" she groaned as she stepped out of the car. She had such a fiery spirit that matched the flaming locks that draped her body. I chuckled.

"And you're stubborn."

I shut her door back and walked her up the school steps. I knew this was the part she hated most. It didn't bother her to make new friends or get acquainted with people; she was a natural. It was the first day when I had to finish signing the paperwork for her enrollment. This is the eleventh school and the eleventh state we had been to since she was old enough to enroll. Word was that Alpha escaped from the Summit and took a massive fleet of angels with him. I knew who their target would be. Me. I opposed him; I was the reason everyone Alpha had turned his back on returned to the Summit.

"Dad, stop thinking. You're frowning, and your face will freeze like that in your old age." Luxina giggled at her joke.

I swooped my arm around her and noogied her head. She pushed me off, straightening her curly locks.

"Trying to have me make a bad impression on the first day with wild woman hair?" Her sarcasm and jokes reminded me so much of her mother.

Before we stepped through the entrance to the school, I stopped to have the talk again. "Remember, keep your wings cloaked at all times.

Make sure you keep your shine under control. If anyone asks, I'm in the military, and you're a spoiled brat who gets whatever you want."

"You mean aside from being able to stay at the schools I wished to."

I narrowed my eyes and frowned at her. She loved irking my nerves on the first day.

"Dad, you don't have to worry. I got this."

Yeah, that's what I thought when she was six, and she decided to show her wings to a little boy in class. *That* was a fun phone call. I ended up having to go and buy a fake pair of wings from the store to produce as the "wings" she showed to him.

We continued through the entrance, and I walked her to the office. A nice young woman met us at the desk. Her eyes lit up when she saw me, and I watched as she messed with her hair to make sure it was straight. Humans always amused me.

"Yes, may I help you?" Her accent had a deep southern tone. I have no clue why I chose to live in Alabama this year.

"Yes, I'm Mr. Graham; I'm here to finish the enrollment paperwork for my daughter, Luxina." She appeared to be a little shocked. My boyish looks always threw them off when I introduced her as my daughter. "I have good genes." I flashed my grin at her, and she blushed.

"Here is the paperwork. We just need a few things to finish up. We received her transcripts, and from her grades and classes, we have placed her in advanced classes." She smiled in approval at Luxina. "You are a very bright young woman." Luxina blushed and dropped her head. She was always self-conscious when it came to compliments about her. "Let's see, we need her birth certificate, her social security number, and a few of your John Hancocks, and we're all set."

I fished her forged birth certificate and social security card out of my wallet and handed them to the secretary. I went through hell trying to get them for her. Finally, I had to use my "powers of persuasion" on the clerk at the courthouse to make up a birth certificate. With the certificate, it was easier to snag a new social for her. I reported she was born at home, and her mother died during the labor. She made copies of both and handed them back. I finished signing the paperwork and slid it back over to the secretary. She looked over everything and placed a stamp of today's date as received. She then went to the computer and printed a piece of paper up, handing it to Luxina.

"Here is your schedule. Do you need a map of the school to find your way around?" Without waiting for a reply, she handed over a map to Luxina. Luxina smiled and murmured her thanks. "I hope you have a good first day, sweetie. Welcome to Decatur, Alabama." She smiled and then looked at me. "It was nice meeting you." I nodded and walked from the office with Luxina.

"I'll be here when the bell rings." I hugged her, and she made her way through the crowd of teenagers.

In reality, she was much younger than everyone thought she was. All angel babies were born in the Summit and adhere to the aging principle there. On Earth, apparently, it was different. She was born on February 6, 2009. She should only be ten years old right now. Luckily, her growth spurt hit in the past couple of years. Most blame it on the hormones when children grow quickly. When her age started rapidly changing, I started bouncing her around from town to town. When she hit around puberty age, her aging slowed again, and it was easier to maintain what her age was. Her birth certificate went from 2009 to 2002, making her seventeen with her birthday coming up.

I made my way out the front entrance of the school when I felt an eerie feeling of someone watching me. I looked around but didn't see anyone. There was a straggler teen making his way up the steps, but other than him, no one else was around. I made my way down the steps when the young man bumped into me. He looked up at me, and I stopped in my steps. His face looked so familiar, though I had never met him before. He had crisp blue eyes, red hair, and pale skin.

"Excuse me," he mumbled, as he continued through to the school.

I continued on my way to my car. *Why did he look so familiar? Maybe his parents were people I went to school with in New Salem.* I nodded, agreeing with the thought. *That had to be it.* I started the car and made my way back to the house. I didn't have to be at work for another couple of hours.

The first couple of years were rough. I was taking care of a baby by myself and trying to work two jobs to save up money. Of course, then, I didn't really need the money. We lived at the Glade, but I knew we couldn't live there forever without the renegade angels looking for us. I saved up enough money from working to where we would always have a decent amount in savings in case we ever had to run. So far, we have been lucky.

As she grew older, the questions started to come. Where was Mommy? Why wasn't Mommy with us? It was hard explaining to a four-year-old the circumstances that surrounded the situation. I told her Mommy was on an important mission, and I didn't know when she would be able to return. I have waited for the question to come up again. I started the car and sighed. I hoped she wouldn't ask me again. This time, I wouldn't be able to make up a story; I would have to tell her the truth. I partially explained the events surrounding Alpha and the renegade angels. She knew the gist of it.

I made my way home with the same eerie feeling I had at the school. Maybe Luxina was right, and I was becoming exceedingly paranoid. I pulled into the driveway of our house and switched the car off. I checked the mail to see if any bills had made it to me yet, but the box was empty, so I made my way inside. I closed the door behind me and went to the kitchen. I put a pot of coffee on and scrounged up some breakfast. It was too obvious for me to remain in my angel form, so I took on the human form I had once been and reassumed the identity of Isaiah. I had coached Luxina to do the same to help hide her identity better. I poured myself a cup of coffee and stood at the window in the kitchen, peering out into the garden Luxina had grown over the summer when we first moved here.

"Whatcha looking at?" I nearly dropped the cup of coffee from my hand when I turned to the voice.

"Lucifer, what are you doing here?" I was immediately on alert looking out the window for any other angels that may be lurking.

"It's just me here," he said, putting the picture down he held in his hands of Luxina. "Who is that?" he asked. I was too startled to answer.

"What are you doing here?" I asked again.

"I wish I could say it's a pleasure visit, but it's not." He walked around the house, looking at all the decorations. He stopped when he came to a picture of Sophie. "Has she been by to see you any?"

"You know the answer to that. I haven't seen her since that night." I set my cup of coffee down, walked into the living room, and sat down. Just when I thought I could get past everything that had happened that night, he showed up at my house. He took a seat in a chair across from me.

"You look good." He was beating around the bush.

"Look, if you've come to ask if I know anything about the location of Alpha, you've come to the wrong place. I haven't heard from or seen anyone since that night." I stood as I heard the oven beep, signaling my breakfast was ready.

"That's only part of the reason I'm here," he said, following me to the kitchen.

"Oh yeah, well, quit beating around the bush and get to it then." He was so annoying when he didn't come right out and say what needed to be said. I pulled the food out of the oven and set it on top of the stove. I started for the refrigerator to get some drinks.

"I'm looking for my son." I stopped in my tracks. *What?* I turned around to face him.

"What do you mean you are looking for your son?" He walked to the table and sat down.

"When we returned to the Summit, Alpha had taken off with a fleet of angels...including my son." I sat down at the table, flabbergasted.

"Do you even know what he looks like? Or, for that matter, where exactly he might be?" I could've passed by this kid one hundred times while I have been here on Earth.

"We've been searching galaxies for him. We always catch a faint sense of him, and then it disappears." He fiddled with a coaster I had on the table.

"By we, you mean Sophie and you, right?" It still stung saying her name aloud.

He sighed. "She misses you, you know?" I looked down at the table. "Mother misses you as well. Xavier keeps them company, though."

I picked my head up and looked at him, puzzled. "Xavier? Who is Xavier?" The look on his face showed he made a slip of the tongue.

"Wow, I feel like kicking myself in the behind now." He shook his head as he realized what slipped from his mouth. "Xavier is...your son." I know the look on my face had shock, surprise, and disbelief written all over it.

"Impossible," I stammered.

"No, it's true. When the portal closed, she found him lying right beneath where it had been. It's actually quite remarkable. He's unlike any angel we have witnessed before. He's been—"

"Growing and aging, unlike any other baby angel." This time, his face showed shock.

"How do you know that?" I walked to the picture of Luxina and picked it up. *Twins?* "Incaendiel, how do you know that?" I held up the picture of Luxina to him.

"Because this is his sister."

His jaw dropped, and he took the picture from my hands. He stared at the picture as if looking at it for the first time. He smiled. "She looks just like her mother." He handed it back to me, and I put it back on the shelf. "Does anyone else know about her?"

I shook my head. "I've been bouncing from town to town so no one could find me or her. I'm surprised Mother doesn't know." I looked back over at him.

"If she does, she hasn't told us. Our main focus has been looking for Damian."

"What does he look like? I might have seen him in one of the towns I've lived in." We sat back down at the table.

"We're not for sure. We only know him as a little baby. If he has the same growth issue as...the twins do, we have no clue what he would look like right now." I nodded and glanced down at my watch.

"Crap! I'm going to be late for work." I ran to get my briefcase from my bedroom. I came back into the kitchen and looked at Lucifer. "Um, make yourself at home. I'll be back after Sophie, I mean, Luxina gets out of school." *Now he has Sophie on my brain. Great! It took me ten years to get her off my mind. Now she's back on it again. Not only that, but I have a son I have never met before...*

Just as I was about to step out the door, the phone rang. I walked over to it and answered it, "Hello?'

"Mr. Graham, we're calling in regard to your daughter, Luxina." *Wonderful! What has she done now?*

"Yes, is anything wrong?" *I was going to beat her if she showed her wings to anyone again!*

"It seems she fainted in class. She's been in the nurse's office for about twenty minutes. She asked us to go home." My heart thudded.

"I'll be right there." I hung the phone up and then dialed the office. "Hey, Margie, it seems Luxina fainted in school, so I won't be coming in today." The call went briskly with her offering her condolences and saying she hoped she felt better.

"Do you want me to ride along to keep you company?" Lucifer grinned. I rolled my eyes. Today was not my day.

"Sure," I said with fake enthusiasm, opening the door of the house.

We walked to the car and drove off to the school. We rode in silence, and the time passed quicker than expected. I put the car in park and walked to the office. The same secretary sat there smiling at me.

"She's through there," she said, pointing to a small hall with a room at the end. I walked to the room, and Luxina was lying on the nurse's bed asleep.

"Hi, you must be her father," the nurse said, extending her hand to me.

"Yes, do you know what exactly happened?" I asked, shaking her hand.

"She was in gym class and fainted, is all we were told. I figured the first day of school at a new school was a bit much for her." She smiled apologetically. "You can sign her out at the front desk. She woke up after fainting, but she went back to sleep." I nodded and walked to the desk to sign her out.

When I came back to the nurse's office, Luxina was sitting up on the side of the bed. The color of her face didn't look good, but that's not what sent the dread through my spine. Her eyes looked frightened.

"Come on, peaches," I said, holding my arm out.

She stood up using my arm, and I wrapped it around her. She walked slowly and groggily out of the school. We went to walk down the steps when she nearly hit the ground again. I picked her up and carried her to the car. I sat her in the backseat and ran around to my door, hopping in.

I put the car in drive and pulled away from the school. "What happened?!" I shouted.

"A boy...in gym class..." she trailed off. Rage erupted through me.

"What boy? What did he do to you?! Did he hurt you, touch you, what?!" I gripped the steering wheel.

"No," she replied. "He showed me his wings."

# CHAPTER 2

I SLAMMED ON THE BRAKES, and the car came to a screeching halt. "What do you mean he showed you his wings? How old is he? What's his name? What does he look like?" I pelted the questions out. Lucifer placed his hand on my arm.

"She's still lightheaded. For now, save the questions."

"No! I must find out right now what's going on. We don't know if it's a renegade angel in human form or what! Luxina," I turned around in my seat, but she had passed out again.

I slammed the car into drive and sped to the house. I threw the car into park and jumped out. I scooped her up from the back seat and walked her into the house. Lucifer ran and grabbed the door. I laid her on the couch in the living room. I looked her over to see if he had done anything to her. It makes no sense why she keeps passing out. Is she frightened or just completely unraveled that more of us exist?

"Lucifer, wet me a washcloth, please. They're in the bathroom. I have to get her to come to so I can see what he's done to her." Lucifer ran to the bathroom and came back with a cold washcloth. I placed it on her face, patting it in circles, trying to get her to wake. She opened her eyes groggily.

"Daddy?" she asked. She must not remember me picking her up from school. *What the hell did this boy do to her?*

"Yes, peaches, it's me. Do you feel like sitting up?" She shook her head, and I could tell the slightest movement of her head sent dizzying waves through her.

"Sweetie, do you remember anything about this boy?"

"At first, he seemed shy. He wasn't talking with the other kids. I thought he was new like me. I started talking to him. It seemed we had a lot in common. He said he had bounced from town to town as well. I asked him his name, and he skirted around it." Lucifer brought her a glass of water from the kitchen, and she sipped on it.

"What did he look like?" I asked patiently.

"He had blue eyes, the bluest eyes I had ever seen, pale white skin, and red hair."

My heart dropped to my feet. That was the kid from the steps that morning.

"He pulled me to a part of the gym where no one could see us. He said he knew who and what I was. I told him I didn't know what he was talking about. That's when he flashed me his wings. He said they were coming for me. No matter where we went, no matter how far we ran, they would find us." I panicked. *What the hell can we do?* "He said he had a message for me to give you."

"What did he say?" I was on full alert now.

"He said to tell you that he said hi. Damian and Alpha say hi."

"Damian!" Lucifer yelled. "He's trained him to be an angel hunter?!" Lucifer began to pace. I sat down on the floor where I kneeled beside her.

"Daddy, who is Damian? Why do they want us? What does this have to do with us?" She was in tears.

"Do you feel up to packing?" I asked. She nodded. "Good, go pack the necessities as I told you. Pack all the pictures of us in the house. We have to leave." She rose from the couch, uneasy at first, but she steadied herself and made her way to her bedroom.

"You have to tell her what's going on. How much have you told her about everything?" I just looked at him. "You haven't told her anything. She couldn't even sense he was an angel, Incaendiel! For Christ's sake!"

"She wasn't ready to know."

"That's not an excuse! She was in danger today and didn't even know it. She needs to know everything, including who Damian is to her!" He was right.

"What do you mean who Damian is to me? What is he talking about, Dad?" I closed my eyes and breathed out. She had walked back in without us knowing. "Dad, who is Damian?"

There was no more hiding it from her. "Damian is your half-brother." Her eyes went wide.

"I have a brother, and you didn't even tell me!" I looked at Lucifer with a "thanks a lot" look. "When were you going to tell me? Is that why Mom left? To have another family?" She looked at Lucifer. "What do you have to do with any of this? Who are YOU?"

"Lucifer is Damian's father." She teared up.

"My mom left us for you!?" She was angry and hurt. "And you! You didn't even think this was important to tell me?! You are my father! You're supposed to protect me, and by protecting me, you need to tell me everything! How could you not tell me this?" She walked over to Lucifer. "Where is my mother?"

"She's off looking for Damian. We've been searching for him for years. He was stolen from us." Lucifer looked nervous. He didn't know what to say. Hell, I didn't know what to say.

"So, this entire time, she has been looking for him. Ten years! She couldn't pop in and say hello. Sorry I abandoned you with your father!" She flopped down on the couch, crying.

"She didn't know you existed," Lucifer said.

"Oh, yeah, that makes me feel even better." She eyed me. "What else have you not told me?"

I sighed. I guess it's time to tell her everything. So, I sat down and told her the entire story beginning at the fall all the way to the portal closing. She cried through the whole time. When I finished, she eyed Lucifer.

"You're the reason she left. If it hadn't been for you, I would have my mom. This is all your fault!"

"No, Luxina, this is all my fault. Don't blame him. Your mother could have never survived without going back to the Summit." She collapsed in my arms, heaving out tears.

"You shouldn't have made her go. I'm fine. She would have been fine, too." The tears welled behind my eyes. *How can I explain to her that she had a family when she's part of her family?*

"Damian needed his mother. This was before I knew about you. I found you after the portal closed. It wouldn't have been fair to keep his mother from him."

She flew off the handle. "Oh, so it's fair that you kept her from me!"

"That's not what I meant. We had no idea that we were going to get you out of this in the end, nor your brother!"

There are moments in life where you smack yourself and think, I shouldn't have said that. At this exact moment, I was kicking myself.

"What do you mean my brother!? You said Damian was born long before I was." I looked to Lucifer, who turned and walked to the kitchen. *Gee, thanks for the help.*

"I found out about your brother right before I picked you up from school. He's your twin." She sat there quietly and red-eyed.

"When will I be able to meet him?" I knew the question was coming.

"Right now, we need to leave and find safety. Then, we will talk about what we can and can't do."

I stood up and ran to my room. I packed a few changes of clothes and walked back through to the living room. She still sat on the couch with the truth of her life sinking in. I felt like a terrible father as if I had let her down. Lucifer stepped outside when I went to pack, getting the car ready to bolt.

"You ready?"

She nodded and stood from the couch. She picked up her duffle bag and walked to the door. I stopped, grabbed the two pictures from the cabinet, and stuffed them in my bag. I heard her open the door and step outside.

"DADDY!" she screamed.

I dropped my bag and ran to the door. As I walked out the door, I was struck from the side. When I regained my vision, my eyes swept across the yard. Beelzebub stood with the boy she named as Damian. He clutched her to his side, holding a knife to her throat. My hands were wrenched behind my back and zip-tied. I looked over my shoulder to see who it was, and my heart crashed. It was Lucifer.

"What the hell, Lucifer?!" I flexed my arms, but the ties were stronger than I thought.

"Alpha promised to return my son if I helped capture your daughter." His face was solemn. Anger flew through me, but he placed a knife against my throat. "Don't think about it, Incaendiel."

"Well, since we all know each other here now, let's get down to business." Damian snickered. I already hated that kid. "Father wants your daughter, and from what I hear, she should be a nice little firebug to add to his collection." He walked over to Luxina. "Hello, Sister. Since now you know the truth, no hard feelings about earlier." She spat in his face, and he smacked her. "Is that any way to treat family?" He turned back to me.

"Lucifer, or should I say 'Dad,' is going to make sure we get away without you hunting us down so soon. What would be the fun in that?" In the blink of an eye, they were gone.

"If I let you out of these ties, do you promise not to kill me?" I was enraged and just nodded my head. He cut me loose, and I socked him in the face. I kept punching and kicking him until he fell to the ground.

"I only promised not to kill you." I kicked him once more and made my way off the porch.

"You will never find her, Incaendiel."

"You don't know me too well then, Brother."

I jumped in my car and drove it until it ran out of gas. I handed the keys over to a homeless man. "Do what you want with it. The title is in the glove box."

I walked to an empty alley and then blinked to the Glade. I dropped my human form and took back my angelic one. I walked to the crest of the mountain, and with every ounce of power in me, I willed the portal open. I stepped through and closed it behind me.

"Metatron!" I yelled out.

My voice echoed through the Summit. All the angels stopped and stared. A figure barreled in front of me from the sky, landing with a loud thud.

"Incaendiel, how the hell did you open the portal? How are you here?" I grabbed him up by his shirt.

"Who all was in on it?" My eyes flared flames.

"No one! I swear. We didn't even know what was going on. I swear." I saw fear flash over his face and dropped him to the ground.

"Where's Sophie? Where's my son?!" I boomed.

"Lucifer locked Sophie in the tower and took off with Xavier." He backed away.

"You were all supposed to protect her, to protect whatever was mine, or did you forget who returned you home!?" The ground shook beneath my feet. "Where's the tower?!" He pointed off to the home that once belonged to Alpha. I flew to it, and the closer I got, the tower came into view.

Metatron flew behind me. "You can't open it. We tried!" I landed in front of the door. I pushed on it, and it didn't budge.

"Where's the key?!"

"Lucifer has it," he replied.

I placed my hand around the cracks of the door and pulled with all my might. The wall around the door began to crack. I pulled harder, and the door gave, breaking a hole in the tower. I stepped through the opening, and there she was, slumped against the wall. I ran over to her and lifted her face to mine.

"Sophie?" She opened her eyes, and a tear slid down her cheek.

"I must be dreaming," she murmured. Her head drooped again as she passed out. I lifted her off the floor and carried her out of the tower. Metatron stood shaking. "Where is Mother?!" I howled.

"When Lucifer went haywire, she fled and hid. She was afraid he would hand her over to Alpha." I swallowed back the anger bubbling up.

I looked at all the angels gathered around me. "I freed you from the purgatory Alpha sentenced you to. I now need your help. He has taken the one thing in my life that left me with any sense of purpose. Who of you will stand with me?" I looked around at all the faces. No one spoke up. "Who will stand with me!?" I yelled louder, and still, no one answered. "I see where loyalty lies with you all." I began walking back to the portal where the mountain was.

"Wait, Incaendiel." Metatron ran up behind me. "I will stand with you." I turned around with Sophie's arms still draped around my shoulder.

"I will, too," Michael said, stepping forth from the crowd of angels.

"We will, too," Samael said as he and Azazel stepped forward. One after another, angels stepped forward, just as we did when we took the fall with Mother.

"Thank you all." I summoned the portal open, and we all stepped forward and back onto Earth. The difference this time, they kept their light. We all descended into the Glade, what was once everyone's home who stood with me. I laid Sophie down in the room I once shared with our daughter. I returned to the meeting room, where everyone waited for a plan of attack.

"How did you know about Xavier?" Azazel asked.

"I didn't until Lucifer told me about him." Everyone looked puzzled.

"How did you know he took him then?" Michael asked.

"Metatron told me when I arrived. I didn't call you together just to save my son. They took something from me that meant the world to me.

The only thing I had left of Sophie in this world. They took my daughter." Michael's eyes went wide, and everyone looked shocked.

"You have a daughter?!" Azazel asked, bewildered.

"When the portal closed, I found her just outside of it. She is Xavier's twin." The room fell silent.

"We have twins?"

The sound of the voice sent chills through my body. I turned around, and Sophie walked through the group of angels. My heart thumped in my chest, and anxiety overwhelmed me. The world stopped around me as she made her way to me.

"What does she look like?" she asked.

"She looks just like you," I murmured.

I wanted to touch her face, to take her in my arms, but I didn't know if I was still allowed to do that. I broke my gaze off her and brought my attention back to the group.

"Does anyone have a way to track Lucifer? I left him in Alabama, and I don't know if he's still there."

"We've heard rumors that Alpha was holed up in Alabama. We don't know if he will trade off locations now that he has been found out or if he will stay and fight." Michael pulled out a map of the state. "Where were you living when they found you out?"

I pointed to the map. "We were living in Decatur."

I could feel Sophie's gaze on me. I couldn't look at her. I was too ashamed. The one person I thought I could trust her with, the one person who was supposed to take care of her and protect her, broke his vow to me.

"Michael, Samael, and Azazel, you're coming with me. We're going to stake out Decatur for any signs of them still hanging around." Metatron's orders came out in the same voice I remembered him always using. He looked over at me. "We will get your kids back. You have my word."

At this point, his word meant more to me than any other person in this room. They took off out of the room and went on their way to Decatur. The other angels made themselves at home once again as they had so many years ago.

Sophie remained in the same spot. I kept my back turned to her. I couldn't look at her face. It pained me knowing she was locked away in that tower again, and it was all my fault. I leaned over the table the map was laying on and traced every part of Alabama in my head. I figured she would leave the room or say something, but I knew she was waiting for me to say something. I bowed my head and took a deep breath.

"I'm sorry, Sophie." I turned around to look at her. Her eyes were trained on me, but they held no emotion. "I didn't know Lucifer would do what he did." I wanted to walk to her and throw my arms around her.

She walked from the room silently. I closed my eyes and inhaled deeply. I followed her back to the room I had placed her in. I watched her as she stared at all the pictures I had on the wall of Luxina as a baby. I cleared my throat. "She looks just like you now."

"What did you name her?" Her voice sounded so familiar and yet, like a stranger's voice at the same time.

"Luxina. She was the only light left in my world of darkness." She touched the picture of her. "What does Xavier look like?"

"He looks just like you. I think that's what made Lucifer lose it. He loved Xavier, and then he started to change. He became angrier and jealous of him. I don't know what sent him over the edge that last day, but he locked me away in the tower and left with Xavier." I watched as a tear slid down her cheek. She looked over at me. "I could have stayed, and none of this would have ever happened."

"It would've eventually happened. Lucifer wants his son back. He doesn't realize what Alpha has turned him into." I walked over to her and wiped the tears from her cheeks that kept coming in multiples. "I would have never let him take your hand if I knew he wouldn't protect you as he promised me."

I pulled her into my chest, and she heaved in sobs. I cradled her in my arms. She pulled back, wiping the tears from her face. I wanted to kiss her so badly. I craved her arms around me, her body around me. Being this close to her brought back the same magnetic pull I had always felt with her.

"Is it too late?" she asked, looking up at me.

"Too late for what?" I was confused.

"For what we had to still be?"

I didn't even bother to answer. I scooped her up in my arms and planted my lips on hers. I expected her to pull back, but she fell deeper into my embrace and kiss. This is what I missed. This is what I lay awake thinking of every night. I had my Sophie back, but look at the cost. I broke away from the kiss with my heart wrenching in two.

"It is too late," she said as she stepped back from me. I pulled her back to me.

"No, that's not it at all."

"Then what is it?" Her eyes pleaded with mine.

"There's a little girl that stole what was left of my heart that needs to be found. I can't do this knowing those monsters have my baby girl."

# LUXINA

# CHAPTER 3

*PULL IT TOGETHER, LUXINA!* Never had I ever had to give myself a pep talk. Then again, I had never been kidnapped by renegade angels. They were the lowest things on Earth, the true definition of demons that had been passed down by the human bible. I awoke shackled in a stone room and smiled to myself. They must think that I don't have any training with my angel abilities. I tried to blink away, but nothing happened. *What the hell?* I tried again with the same results. I didn't understand. I tried to break the shackles, which was pointless. All that got me was two bruised wrists. I turned around and pulled with all my might, trying to get them to break from the wall. Nothing gave; nothing broke, so I slumped against the wall.

"You won't be able to break them," a voice said from the far wall of the room. It was dark, so I squinted to see who the voice was.

"How do you know? Who are you? Why do they want me?" I tried to sound strong in my words, but my emotions were slipping out.

"I know because I've tried. They have unicorn hair melted in the metal. We can't escape unicorn hair." I heard his chains begin to clank. He walked from the dark corner he had been sitting in to where the slight crack of light came into the room. "I'm Xavier. I would shake your hand, but as you see, I, too, am shackled to the wall. As to why they want you, I have no clue. What's your name?" He sat down in the light so I could still see him. It wasn't enough light to completely illuminate his face, but his voice sounded kind and caring, almost as if I had heard it before.

"My name is Luxina. How long have you been here?" I, too, sat down against the wall, still watching him.

"It's hard to say the amount of time I have been

here. Barely any light filters through here, and I'm not used to Earth's hours of light. If I had to guess, I've been here all summer."

"Who had you kidnapped?" I still can't believe Lucifer betrayed those in the Summit. I mean, when you think about it, you honestly can't blame the guy. He was trying to get that asshole of a brother of mine back.

"I was kidnapped by Lucifer. They're handing me over to Alpha for the release of Damian." I heard him snort in anger.

"That's exactly why they kidnapped me!" A few moments of silence went by. I didn't know what else to ask or say to him, and I assume he felt the same way.

"Can I ask you something?" His voice, the more I heard it, the more it sounded familiar to me, like the dreams I had growing up.

"What do you want to know?"

"Do you remember me?" I felt like the breath was knocked from my lungs.

"Um, not really. Your voice sounds familiar, but I can't really see your face."

"We've played together in our dreams since we were babies. Mother told me there were no angel babies in the Summit with the name Luxina, but here you are." I could hear the smile in his voice.

"I'm not from the Summit. I was born and raised on Earth by my dad." Every hour away from him, I missed him terribly.

"Is your dad a human?" I chuckled at the question.

"No, he used to be an angel at the Summit. He took the fall when the Dark Mother did and, long story short, sacrificed his angelic light for the others to make it back into the light."

"Your dad is Incaendiel, right?" His voice sounded like it perked up a bit.

"Yes."

"Damian is your half-brother, too, right?"

At first, I was a little stunned to hear that he knew that. "Yes."

"Your mom is Sophie."

"Ok, now you're scaring me. How do you know all this?"

"Well, apparently, you're my sister as well. Your parents are my parents; aside from I've never met my dad." My jaw dropped. I had only just learned about either of them even existing. Now, I have met both of them?

"How do I know you're not lying to trick me? How do I know you're not feeding me this crap to get close to me and find out information for them?!"

"You have to trust me, Luxina. No one in the Summit aside from me knew about another angel named Luxina. We've had a connection in our dreams for years. There must be a reason why. My mother and father are the same people you named. They didn't have kids until that portal was opened and closed. They found me in the Summit, where the portal closed. I've never met my father; I've only heard about him. My grandmother told me about him every day."

"I don't believe you. You're just trying to get under my skin and find out information for them. Stop talking to me!" Tears had started to fall. I had only learned I had a twin brother this morning, and now, he wants to lay claim to that title. This had to be a trick. The angels in the Summit would not have let him be kidnapped. I heard his sigh, breaking me from my thoughts.

"When you were three, we met in a meadow in a dream. A beautiful meadow I have never laid eyes on. At first, we spoke no words to each other. We just stood and stared at each other, frightened of one another."

"Stop."

"I walked closer to you, and you backed away.

You tripped and fell backward. I reached for your hand to help you stand, and our powers collided, leveling the valley."

"Stop."

"I stared you in the eyes, and I told you to take my hand. You would always be safe with me in the dreams. I kissed you on your forehead."

"Stop! That's enough! Quit trying to use my dreams against me! You are not the little boy I have been meeting in my dreams. It's not possible!"

He went silent. I was silent. *How could they take such personal thoughts of mine and try to use them against me to gain my trust? It's horrible!*

"Through the mountains and over the sea, the firefly will cease to be." I looked at him as he continued. "Over the valley and through the meadow, the firefly exists in the shadows." My breathing got faster. There is no way anyone knows this poem. "Fly away, firefly, until we meet again. Maybe next time, it won't be a dream that I get to hold your hand." My heart was racing. *It can't be. He can't be the boy in my dreams.*

"How do you know that poem?" I retreated as far as I could to the wall I stood before.

"You're my firefly."

"You can't be him. He's not real, and you

certainly can't be my brother."

"We're more than just that, Luxina. We're soulmates. The Dark Mother told me that we must be like Mom and Dad. We were created as one soul and split, and only a tremendous amount of power could have created us."

"Aw, isn't that sweet? The two of you are getting reacquainted." The lights flickered on, and Damian walked in. He glanced over at Xavier. "I should have known everyone, including our grandmother, would have favored you over me."

My eyes fell to where Xavier sat, and I sucked in a sharp breath. It was him, the boy that existed only in my dreams. Dad always told me that he wasn't real but just a dream. I held onto the belief he was real. He had to be real. His face and heart always called to mine. Whenever I was with him, him sheltering me from the world, I felt safer and a little more. My heart fluttered when his eyes met mine.

"Father has plans for you two. Of course, I don't know what they are," he turned to face me and smiled, "but he said I could do whatever I wanted with you two beforehand, aside from killing you, that is." He walked closer to me and ran his finger along my jawline. I moved my head away from his touch, cringing. His touch disgusted me.

"Don't touch her." It was a simple statement, but I could feel the emotion behind the growl that escaped his lips. It sent shivers and chills down my spine.

"The one in chains decides to give me orders. That's quite funny." He walked over to Xavier and backhanded him. I watched as he pulled against the chains, standing up against Damian. I could see the fury in his eyes. "If you weren't so goody-two-shoes, we could've been best buds, but no, you're a mama's boy."

"Don't forget your place, Damian, and mind the words you say. My mother is your mother as well."

"Yeah, and look what she did. She left me and my father behind, my real father, to go screw yours." I could see the anger building in Damian's face as the words left his mouth. The boys stood staring each other down with equal looks of hatred.

"Alpha tells you lies! Our mother has spent the last ten years searching for you. She has spent more time looking for you than what she did raising me! If anyone should be jealous of the other, it would be me. I'm a bigger person. I love my brother no matter what! I wished every day for your safe return!" *I don't think I could ever love Damian.* "I can tell you this, though: you lay another finger on her, and you won't have to worry about mother loving you anymore."

His eyes pierced into Damian's eyes. My breath caught in my lungs. Aside from my dad, no one has ever stood up for me in that way. I watched a wicked grin tug at the corners of Damian's mouth.

"Unlike our stupid mother, she can be broken down. Father has thought this through better than what he did last time." He turned back around to face me. "I will be seeing you soon." He walked to the door and left, leaving the light on. My eyes trailed back over to Xavier, who was wiping the blood from the corner of his mouth.

"Are you okay?" I asked. It came out with more concern than what I thought I felt.

"I'll live. He hits like a girl." I couldn't help but giggle. He just stared at me. "I can't believe it's really you," he murmured.

I could feel the heat rush to my cheeks. Boys never looked at me like that; either that or I never noticed they did. He continued to stare at my face with wonder in his eyes.

"I can't believe you remember the poem. I used to lay awake at night and run it through my head repeatedly. For the longest time, I thought you were a ghost that haunted my dreams, and here you are."

A smile formed on my face as I looked at him. He was gorgeous. Black hair and the prettiest blue eyes I had ever seen, he was a picture of perfection. I couldn't tear my eyes off him, and it seemed he had the same problem. I snapped my focus back to the problem at hand.

"What do you think he means Alpha thought this through better this time? How am I unlike our mother? How am I weaker?"

"I can only speculate the meaning behind that. Mom devised a plan to help the others return from the fall. The love our parents shared went beyond space and time. No matter how many angels Alpha sent or how many times she incarnated, the only person who had her heart, in the end, was our father." I thought back to the story Dad had told me earlier. I hadn't realized how much of a romantic story it was.

"Well, what about Lucifer? He won over her heart, and he's on their side." I watched as fury flashed through his face.

"Lucifer was not always on their side. He became so engulfed in finding Damian he didn't care what the cost would be. He may have stolen a slight piece of our mother's heart, but our father was the one person that she would level the universe for." *So, there is still hope for their unison.* A warm feeling rushed through my heart hearing that.

"So, how am I different? How am I weaker?" The statement still troubled me. I know I'm a strong-willed person. I take that back; Dad says I'm stubborn and act just as my mother did.

"Our mother and father got a chance to exist together in the Summit before the fall. We have not. We have only met in dreams. We do not share the same bond they do because we have never touched one another. Our bond has not been forged yet; therefore, you are weaker than our mother and more susceptible to the charm of Damian." I cringed at the sound of his name.

"I don't believe that the last part is true. Damian gives me the creeps." I got the heebie-jeebies just thinking of his face. Not that he wasn't good-looking, he had all the charm in that department he needed, but I could feel his sinister side. "What happens if Damian does get under my skin?"

He looked at me, staring at me. "The war would start, the official war, and you would be on their side while I fight for this side. In the end, ultimately, if I cannot save your heart...I must..." He couldn't even finish the sentence. He just looked at me with tears glistening in them. "It won't ever come to the latter, so there's no need to say it." He offered me a warm smile, but I could tell he forced it past the emotion welling in him.

I wish I knew what it felt like in real life and not in dreams, what it was like to touch his hand. I remember the power we shared in our dreams. Could it be any more powerful than that? The more I looked at him, the more I knew he was right. I could feel his heartbeat along with mine. I got lost in his eyes every time they met mine. I could never get over the way he looked at me, as if I was the only person in the entire world.

"What's the other alternative?" He stared at me.

"Have you ever heard what came after the creation story?"

"No, just the search for the Garden." He frowned at me. I bet he was running through his head why on earth didn't our father tell me more.

"After Lilith, our Grandmother Omega, left the Summit, Alpha no longer had the power to create human life the way they did together. Without the combined power of them together, his creations came out mutated, vile, and malevolent. That's why Eve was created from a rib as opposed to the way Adam had been made. The mutations were savage beasts that roamed the earth with blood lust. He had long been experimenting on several types of creatures, trying unusual ways to breed them. He branded them all as demons."

"Yeah, Dad told me that Lilith warned them that he would make the Fallen ones out to be evil as opposed to just fallen angels," I remarked.

Xavier nodded. "The first to be made was what you call vampires. Their thirst for blood outnumbered the animals of the planet that thrived. Alpha tried to destroy the savage monsters and dispatched a sentinel army of his first in command. There were a number of Seraphims, Cherubims, and Thrones sent down to take care of the problems that the beasts were causing. It turned into a blood bath. Alpha had tried making humanity stronger and more agile in his attempts by himself. It increased their strength, but it came with a consequence. The blood lust that frenzied them made incisors develop whenever fresh blood was around. They dropped the army one by one, turning them as well. The angels that were turned didn't become the frenzy of creatures that had turned them."

"What happened to them afterward?" I asked.

"The angels were to become known as the Watchers. Disgraced by their new state of being and unable to return to the Summit, they went underground to what is now called Stygia. They hid from the sight of their Father, damning themselves to the darkness for what they had been made into. When they finally emerged from the darkness and were sensitive to the light's power, they vowed they would hunt down the creatures that had made them the way they were, half-angel half-demon."

"What happened next? Did he send more angels to fight them?" I asked.

"No. Since the best of Alpha's angels couldn't thwart the actions of the humans with fangs, he created another type of horror. He took the blood of hellhounds and created what we know as werewolves. The beasts not only had a blood lust as their enemy, but they killed in more numbers. Not only did they drink the blood of their kill, but they ate the bodies as well. Unpleased by his efforts in creating these creatures, Alpha cursed the beasts in three ways. The first way, whoever survived the malicious attacks of the beasts became one as well. They would shift during the full moon into their form, as opposed to remaining the beast like the originals were, cursing them further into damnation, being neither human nor beast. The third curse was that they all would bear the mark he would later call the Mark of Cain. The Mark of Cain is a blessing and a curse all in one. Whoever tries to harm the creatures would be struck down by hellfire."

"How awful," I murmured.

"I'm sure you have heard some version of Lott in Sodom and Gomorra, right?"

I nodded my head.

"Well, the stories circulating aren't nearly as close to what really happened. There was a band of werewolves running rampant through the valleys. They were growing closer to the city of Sodom and Gomorra, leaving a trail of bodies in their wake. The city had started gathering the virgins of the city as an offering to the beasts so they would go unscathed. Grandmother caught wind of what was happening and dispatched a few of the Fallen Ones to the city. They went to every house, warning them that their actions would lead to hellfire and brimstone. None wanted to listen to their warnings. Lott was the last house they were to go to. They convinced him of the danger of sacrificing his daughter to the monsters and the impending doom of the city."

"Is that when they decided to leave?" I asked.

"Yes. They fled as the monster struck the center of the city. The girls had been gathered in the center, and instead of killing their offering, they stole their offering for breeding. This made Alpha angry at the city for their stupidity in offering virgin women to these beasts. He poured down the fire on the city as Lott and his family ran."

"Then how did Lott's wife turn into a pillar of salt?" I asked.

"Trailing on their heels were a few stragglers that were still scoping the city out for fresh meat. The Fallen Ones tried their best to keep the stragglers from reaching Lott's family. One slipped away and went nipping at the feet of Lott's wife. She went to smack the beast, turning around to fend it off from herself and before her hand brushed the beast, she was struck by the hellfire and turned to a pillar of salt."

"So, what happened to the werewolves after Sodom and Gomorrah?" I asked.

"The Fallen Ones were eventually able to drive the non-shape shifting beasts to the end of the earth, but not before they met their sworn blood enemies, the vampires."

"What happened when the two different species came into contact?" I asked.

"It was war in itself from the frenzy of the two different bloodlines colliding. Neither could kill the other, something Alpha had never expected when he created them. Their blood only combined, making a more problematic creature than what they had been dealing with. When you take two immortal creatures and mix their blood, one with no heart and the other with a heart, you create an undead creature. The dead began to rise in numbers, warrior creatures that only had primal instinct and couldn't think for themselves."

"Zombies?" I asked flabbergasted.

"Modern culture dubbed these horrors as zombies, but the truth of them has trickled away through time. The Fallen Ones spent years eradicating the vile things from the earth. It was after the slaughter of these unnatural creatures that they finally drove the two enemies apart. They drove the rogue vampires into what we now know as the abyss and the rogue werewolves into Tartarus, where they remained as what they had been created from: hellhounds."

"Wait, but there are still legends of werewolves. Like, among the Native American tribes, they have

116

the Wendigo and Skinwalkers," I replied.

"I will get to that part in a bit. Let me tell it how it happened," Xavier said with a smile.

"Ok," I replied.

"What these beasts left in their wake was catastrophic, but apparently, not catastrophic enough for Alpha. He found the rogue Fallen Ones that darkness had consumed and offered them a deal. If they would help him out when it came down to the final war of the Summit, he would restore their light. These Fallen Ones had been called the Forsaken and such from their name; you can imagine they were more than eager to accept the deal. The Forsaken were to be known as Greater Demons. They later kidnapped humans, feeding them their blood and created minions for themselves, the Lower Demons."

"So, even though Alpha had abandoned them originally and was the cause of them turning dark, they fell right into rank with him?" I asked.

Xavier nodded. "As they patiently waited for Alpha to declare the official war, they became antsy and bored. They decided to start experimenting the same way Alpha did. They took the blood of the Seelies they caught and mixed it with their blood, creating sirens and mermaids. They were as beautiful and lustrous as angels were but nasty and deadly as the vampire, and demon blood coursed through their veins. Once satisfied with their marvelous success, they moved on to the werewolves that inhabited Tartarus. When they mixed their blood together, they created what are known as shapeshifters. These shifters weren't as savage and mindless as the other werewolves were but could shift into anything they wished at any time during the moon cycle. They were like their human half-breed counterpart, but more powerful and deadly since the demon blood coursed through their veins with that of the angel blood."

"So, they are the legends I spoke of?" I asked.

"Yes, and when Alpha found out what his First in Command of the Dark Army had done, he punished him, but even though it was done without his say, he welcomed his children of darkness with open arms. He took the blood of these creatures, the damned, the children of the night writhing with demon blood, and created an elixir with it. He waited for millenniums for the right angel to prove their worth to him, to receive the elixir and become more than just a first in command. Then, to his delight, Lucifer and our mother gave him his final wish. Neither of them could refuse to hand over the baby because they were locked away in the tower. He began experimenting at once on Damian. He didn't mutate or morph because he was already an angel. Instead, he became an angel with demon blood searing through his veins, darkening his heart."

"How do you know all this?" I asked.

"You learn to listen when there is nothing to do except be chained to a wall," Xavier replied.

"Well, what does all that have to do with you and me?" I asked, terrified of his response.

"Because we're different than other angels. He either wants to inject us, then take our blood and use it for Damian or inject the same elixir in us to see what we change into."

"Why? Why are we so different from the others?" My bottom lip had started to tremble.

"We're basically demi-gods."

"How can we be demi-gods? You mean, like Hercules, right? Well, Hercules was half human and half God in the myths. We're not!" I stammered.

"We're not demi-gods in the sense of myths. We're demi-gods in the sense of power our parents had in our creation. We're half-angel and half-god, something no one has ever witnessed before.

Something Alpha is extremely interested in."

"So, what do we do? I don't want him taking my blood for Damian, and I certainly don't want to become some...THING...a laboratory experiment where I end up growing fur, fangs, and can sing songs like Disney characters." I started to rattle my chains and pull on them. I wanted to get OUT of this place. They were not going to use me as some sort of hypothesis where they don't know the outcome's answer.

"Luxina, calm down! It's going to be all right, I promise. You can't get out of those chains. I have already told you that." He was talking calmly and patiently to me. Well, no, he was talking at me.

"Don't patronize me! We're stuck in here and could become monsters and you want me to calm down!" I started breathing deep gulps, trying to stay calm while he just watched me have my nervous breakdown. "What are we going to do then?" I asked breathlessly.

"The only thing we can do... wait."

# CHAPTER 4

I AWOKE from the dark voids of my eyelids. I didn't even remember falling asleep, let alone having a dreamless sleep. I have never experienced sleep without some form of dreaming involved. The dreamless sleep wasn't what captivated my attention; it was the banging of a door as it flew open and hit the wall behind it. I fought the urge to drift back off to sleep as I watched two men drag a body into the room. I could tell it belonged to a female by the black hair that silhouetted the face it hid. I watched as they walked her body by her feet and head to a cot that sat in the corner. I didn't remember the cot being in here, so undoubtedly, they must have come in here once before and brought it in to set it up.

They shackled her hand to one side of the cot that had chains binding it to the floor and wall. They laid her gently in the bed and brushed her hair off her face. To my relief, they stalked out of the room without paying me any attention and shut the door behind them. My eyes trailed back over to the woman sleeping on the cot. Words couldn't describe the beauty that she held. Her black hair had a shimmer to it like the sun hitting glitter. Her skin was the creamiest pale I had ever seen. My gaze drifted from her to Xavier as a feeling gnawed at the pit of my stomach. I glanced in between them noticing they had the same hair color, the same pale skin. *Is this my mother?* I wondered.

"Xavier." He didn't move. *Had they drugged us somehow?* "Xavier," I said a bit louder. He still sat slumped against the wall, asleep. "Xavier!" I hissed, and he stirred. I watched as he fought to open his eyes groggily and look at me. "Who is that?" I asked, motioning my head to the bed. His head shakily trailed in the direction I pointed, and he bolted upright.

"Grandmother! Grandmother, are you ok?!" Worry and fear streaked across his face.

"That's our grandma?!" I breathed. That's when I noticed how similar she and my father looked.

"This is not good, this is not good at all," he murmured and thought inwardly to himself. "Who knows what Alpha has planned or what he intends with all of us."

The woman he called Grandma began to stir on the bed. She sat up from the bed and rubbed her head as if it were sore. When she lifted her eyes, they met mine and went wide. She then turned her head and looked at Xavier. "Xavier, what are you and your mother doing here?"

"She's not my mother, Grandmother, she's not Sophie," he replied.

"She looks just like her!" she exclaimed.

"This is the girl I told you about from my dreams. This is Luxina, my twin sister." The woman stared over at me wide-eyed.

"Are you sure? No one knew you had a sister. Are you sure this isn't a trick?" She glared at me, and I returned the glare back.

"It's not my fault you all abandoned my father and me here once you went back to the Summit. Ten years. It's been ten years, and not a damned one of you checked on him. You didn't make sure he was ok or see if he was still alive. You left us!" I didn't expect that to roll out, but all the emotion I had been holding back since Dad told me everything boiled under my skin. "How hard would it have been for someone to come look in on him? Make sure that he was ok after everything he did to get you back to the Summit." Tears streamed down my face.

"It was too risky to leave the Summit. We didn't know what Alpha had planned once he escaped." She was calm and collected.

"No, it was too risky to check on him, where you would have found out about me, but it wasn't too risky to look for that filthy brother of mine, Damian. The golden boy that everyone put up on a pedestal to find. The one who kidnapped me from my father! I don't even know what happened to him after he blinked me away. I have no clue if he is alive or dead. I have been the lost child of the light for years, and my father spared me the reasoning behind it. I see it now. Even if you were to know about me, I wouldn't have abandoned him here in this forsaken world to go with you all. The 'all-knowing' power didn't know about me. How do we know you're not the trick? You should know everything! You should be able to still feel his emotions. Why don't you?!" Xavier stole a glance at me and then looked back at Lilith sitting on the side of the bed. No emotion fluttered in her face, no retort, nothing.

"Grandmother, are you ok?" Xavier asked, peering closer at her. She didn't move or respond. She just stared blankly ahead. "Grandmother?"

She turned away from our eyes and rolled on her side on the bed. She didn't respond to his repetitive name-calling. Soon, he fell silent and looked at me. I couldn't quite grasp if he was mad at me or not. He just sat there and stared at me.

"Maybe she's right," he spoke softly.

"Right about what?" I asked back.

"Maybe you are a trick of the mind." The breath caught in my throat. It felt like a hammer hit my heart as I heard his statement.

"Me, the trick of the mind. ME! How do I know you're not!? That brat brother of yours dragged me away from my father. How do I know you didn't have a part of it? How do I know if anything you told me is real?! How do I know you're not Alpha disguised and my real brother, XAVIER, isn't locked away somewhere else? Someone drugged me so I wouldn't dream so that I couldn't communicate with him. How do I know you didn't?"

"I refuse to answer your questions. Grandmother is right. You're not her." I was baffled. A moment ago, he was trying to break his chains to go after Damian and now he doesn't want to believe who I am.

"Apparently, we're not the twins. Twins would know one another. Earlier, you had me stupefied into believing you were him, playing on what I had just been told by my father, Lucifer, and Damian. Now...now I don't even know who I am. Since I'm not who I'm supposed to be then what would you care if Damian draws me to his side? I'm nothing special to anyone but my father."

I sat back with tears glistening in my eyes. I didn't care anymore what may or may not happen. Maybe none of this was real. Maybe this whole room was an illusion. All he did was stare at me, and I wanted him to stop. I flicked my hand to the light bulb, and it sparked and blew to where there was darkness in the room. It was the darkness I was accustomed to by being around my father. He showered me in love, and if darkness existed in his soul, then love existed in the dark.

I slipped back against the wall and sank. No one would understand what we have been through for the past ten years. We were always on the run, moving from town to town so no angels would find us, and now look. I've been captured and thrown into a room where both people in here are trying to tell me I'm not who I am. If it weren't for the fact that I'm only ten years old but look like a teenager, I would believe them. I know when I was born, where I was born, and to whom I was born, and no one can tell me any different from that.

"How did you make the light bulb blow?" the voice called out in the dark. I didn't want to answer; I was done talking. "Could you turn it back on? I don't like the dark." His voice sounded meek and guarded.

"Maybe you wouldn't be afraid of it if you hadn't lived your entire life in the light. I'm used to the dark, and it doesn't bother me. You got to live in the Summit. You got to experience the actual touch of the light. Me, I've been shrouded in darkness my whole life. I'm my father's light, the only light he needs. If I'm not the person you thought I was, and you're not the person I thought you were, why should I care?"

"Please." I have never met anyone who could be this afraid of the dark. I flicked my hand, and the bulb sprang back to life with a new energy current. Xavier sat in the corner, hunkered like a little kid.

"There, happy now?" I rolled my eyes in irritation.

"How can you do it?" he asked.

"Do what?"

"Live in darkness for so long." I had never thought of this to myself really. It was just a natural thing I was accustomed to.

"Apparently, I didn't deserve to be in the light as you."

It was a simple answer, but it packed a punch deep within. *Is that what I really think?* Dad always told me I was a gift to him, that I was the light he couldn't have back. I love my dad, but it really wasn't fair to me. I had no choice. I have never had a choice about anything: where we lived, who I could hang out with, nothing. Xavier stared at me as I sat against the wall, pulling my knees to my chest. Of course, I was right. I was being punished for what my parents did. I wasn't supposed to have been created. There wasn't supposed to have been any light left once everyone returned.

I have never felt this lonely and unhappy before. Sinking into depression has never been my thing. I have always been happy and bubbly, but locked away in this room without my dad, everything was sinking in for face value. I wasn't supposed to have been created.

"Why do you think you weren't supposed to have been created?" I looked over to the woman sitting on the side of the bed, staring at me.

"How do you know what I was thinking?" I asked, biting back the tears after hearing the phrase said aloud. She stared at me, the same stare that Xavier had been giving me. "I didn't say that out loud. How did you know I was thinking it?"

"Just because no one knew you existed doesn't mean you weren't meant to exist. You are right; you are the shining light keeping your father afloat. Without you, he had no reason to live. You gave him that tiny ray of hope that one day, you two would come to the Summit. You two are more alike than you think but total opposites as well: you being the light, he being the dark. If I had known you were born, I would have held you as I did all the other grandchildren I have been given. I'm sorry no one was there for you besides your father.

He did an excellent job alone, though," she said, winking at me.

"Grandmother, don't let her get into your head. It's what they want," Xavier piped up. "She will deceive you in any way she can, especially by mimicking the powers of people." He glared over at me. "You may fool others, but you will not fool me."

"Well, I see things went south faster than what I expected," Damian said, walking through the door. "Since you're no longer overly fond of our dear sister, maybe you won't mind if I take her for a little while." He walked over to me and smiled. He reached his hand out and stroked my cheek. "Let's get you out of these chains, shall we?" He removed my manacles and pulled me gently along behind him.

"What are you going to do with her?" Lilith asked.

"Shh, it's a secret." He grinned ear to ear. My eyes flitted from her face to Xavier's face. There was no expression on his, just a blank stare. "Come now, sister, we wouldn't want to keep Father waiting."

He led me from the room with Lilith protesting against my departure. The corridors were gloomy with barely any light filling the space. In the rooms

130

we passed by, I heard screaming and moaning as people shouted out with what could only be torturous pain.

"Those are the ones caught that defy Alpha," Damian said as I shut my eyes, trying to drown out the screams. He led me up a flight of stairs and snaked his way through more halls while I kept my head down, trying to fight off the sounds of the screams erupting from each room we passed. Finally, we arrived at a door at the end of the hall, and we walked in without knocking.

"Father, I brought Luxina to see you," Damian said, shutting the door behind us. The room felt empty and cold. My eyes grazed over all the empty walls and landed on the desk sitting in the middle of the room. Behind the desk sat an old man with silver hair and a smile splattered on his face.

"Hello, Luxina. I have waited ten years to meet my new granddaughter. If you're anything like your parents, you must be a star on the rise. I have never come across two angels that had the power they did, and I must say, I was astonished as well as surprised to learn that their power created you and your brother." He got up from his desk and walked over to me. He placed his arms gently on my shoulders and looked me over. "You are a radiant child." He smiled and then drew me in for a hug. "Now, I bet you're wondering why I went to the lengths I did to bring you to see me. Your father has been angry with me for years, and I doubted he would bring you to me for you to meet me. I hope they have been treating you properly. If anyone has stepped out of bounds, let me know, and they will be punished."

He motioned with his arms to a chair that I can only assume he wanted me to sit in. I obliged and sat down as he walked back around to the other side. Damian took a seat on the wall away from the table. I nervously glanced between the two of them. Neither made any indication they wanted to hurt me or cause any type of torture that I heard as I passed through the halls.

"Is that all you wanted was to see me?" I asked boldly.

"As I said before, I had never come across two angels with the power that your parents share. I wanted to see firsthand what kind of power lay dormant within their children. You and your brother are special; I hope you know that. Neither of you are full angel, human, or anything. You are, how should I say this...you are higher ranked than the Seraphims in the Summit. I'm sure you have heard of demi-gods." Well, Xavier was right about one thing. I nodded my head. "Well, we can't call you a demi-god because you aren't half-human. I have decided to call you two fey."

"Fey? Like in faeries?"

"You are far more superior to faeries. Legend says that the fey were direct creations of the Gods of the mythos, placing them among earth as faeries. It's partially true; they were created by Gods. Even your parents do not know there are other powers as abundant as your grandmother and me, but there are. Where we come from, we haven't the slightest idea, but we exist. However, what separates you from the faeries on earth is that you were created by two angels that had the powers of Gods. Your grandmother created your parents with, as she said, a bit more love added. In truth, she mixed part of her power in with them. They both were our favorites. We always allowed them into the Garden to roam and have fun. They were so light-hearted, but both deadly with their power. When your father fell, it felt right that they be split apart. That much power together was too catastrophic for them to even grasp. It saddened me to learn that your mother was part of a revolution against me. I'm not so bad. She suggested her own punishment and took to it. I was never mad with her or with your father. It was quite the opposite watching these two combine their powers together to complete the task they set out in the beginning to accomplish.

"When they created you two, I was baffled with the product. I could feel the power radiate through the heavens when you two sparked into being. I knew immediately what you had become. You are more than just angels with godlike powers. You are lower-level gods, in between demigods and gods. The angel blood that runs through you is just as remarkable as the godlike powers that do. You are fey, and your children's children will be as well. You two were created for each other just as your parents were, but you are more powerful than just simple twin flames. You two will change everything in this universe together, and I want to be there to witness it."

"That's all...you don't want anything from us?" It was stupid to ask, but I was curious.

"Actually, now that you have asked, there is something you could do for me. I would love to examine your blood, see if it can be replicated or if you are one of a kind spontaneous creation."

"No." I was flat with my answer.

"I would never hurt you, child. Look at your other brother, Damian. I have done no wrong by him." I glanced over at Damian sitting somberly in his chair. He gave a halfhearted smile, but I could see something eating away at his thoughts. When our eyes connected, it was as if I could hear him tell me not to do it.

"No, I don't want to be a laboratory experiment."

"Well, with your permission or without your permission, I will either get what I want from you, or I will cause you days of pain with my own injections to make you more...powerful." Xavier was right. He would turn us into something else.

"My answer is still no. I know more than what you think about all this. You will not get my blood. If you had the power to duplicate us, you would have already. For all I know, you want to take our blood for him," I said, motioning to Damian, who looked tired and weary.

"Well, I see cooperation is not in the works here. Damian, take her back to the cell and have the men start immediately working on her. I want the results documented and blood work each day after the injections." Alpha looked over at Damian who at first looked as if he were to say no as well. He glanced at me once more, and I could definitely see the noticeable pain in his eyes that time.

"Yes, Father, as you wish." He stood and walked over to me, tugging at my sleeve to stand.

"Excellent." Alpha flicked us away with his hand. Damian pulled me from the room, and we started back down the halls.

"I'm sorry, Luxina." It was the only thing he said to me, and I didn't respond. I knew he had no choice but to listen to the only person he knew as a father. I would obey my father as well.

When we returned to the room, there was a bed set on the side of the room I had been in. I watched as Lilith looked me over to see any signs of trauma while I had been gone. Damian bent down, picked up a manacle, and laced it back around my wrist.

"I'll be the one to check on you each day." He held my hand and squeezed it lightly then let it drop to my side.

I sat down on the bed as he walked from the room. I didn't know how these injections were going to go. All I knew was he wasn't getting untainted blood from me. I looked over at Lilith, who sat nervously on the bed. My eyes skimmed over to Xavier, who still hadn't moved from his seat.

136

"You were right, Xavier," I whispered.

"Right about what?" he asked. Two men walked into the room, pushing a cart with syringes on it. I looked from the cart and back to him.

"Lie back on the bed, and this will go smoother," one of them said. I obeyed and lay back on the bed. I felt the sting of the needle as they injected one of the syringes. They followed suit with four more and then left the room.

"Luxina, what are they injecting you with?!" Lilith hissed. I couldn't answer. I was already beginning to feel the dull ache wash over me. "Luxina!"

I drifted off into space. I didn't pass out. I was aware of everything. I could hear my name being yelled at to get my attention. I couldn't respond when I tried to answer. It wasn't as bad as I thought it would be. I began to drift deeper into an unconscious state. My name became less audible until it felt like I was in utter silence and complete darkness.

# CHAPTER 5

AT FIRST, it felt like a bee was stinging me. I figured the men had come back in and were giving me more injections. The bee sting feeling grew in intensity to where it felt like a knife was digging into my arm. The pain started radiating from my arm and through my body. It felt like I was being stabbed repeatedly. A hot sensation filled my body along with the stabbing. I felt like I was being thrown into a crematorium, and fire was searing my flesh. I knew from biology that once the fire burns your nerves, the pain subsides before you die. In my case, the hot, fiery pain didn't leave.

Instead, an icy hot feeling enveloped me as well. I felt like I couldn't breathe. I tried to swallow, but it felt like hot coals trickled down my throat instead of saliva. It felt like lava sprang from my tear ducts as I cried the pain out.

I writhed in pain. There was no relief from it, no momentary give to the searing flesh. I thought I was going to die from sheer agony. My body started to convulse, and I felt my hands flailing against the wall hard. I don't know if I was actually hitting the wall or not, but even the sensation in my hands didn't register a new pain. The burning, stabbing pain overwhelmed any of my other sensory functions.

I didn't know how long the pain had lasted, but it finally began to subside. My eyes opened and burned in the light above me. A blurry shadow hovered over me, and when I finally focused, Damian was bent over me, mouthing words. Apparently, my senses hadn't come back yet. I tried to sit up, but the world felt like it was raining hellfire around me when I lifted any limbs to move. My hearing started to return in a low, shrill hum. It grew louder and shrill, as if someone were blowing a whistle. When it reached normal hearing capacity, I realized it wasn't a whistle but my own screams being muffled.

"Luxina!" Damian yelled. He touched my arm, and pain shot through it, sending another scream from my lips.

"Stop touching her! You're making it worse!" another voice boomed out. I couldn't recognize the voice through all the pain and ringing in my ears from my own screams of anguish.

"I have to make sure she stays conscious. She wasn't supposed to have a blackout like that! Luxina, it's Damian. Say something, anything!" I tried to respond, to croak something out, but even my throat was so dried out and hoarse from the screaming it didn't want to cooperate like everything else. "She can't do these injections. They are literally killing her."

"What do you freaking care?!" the voice yelled out again.

"She's my sister. I care!" Damian yelled back. "I'm going to Father at once to report this. I will return in a few minutes." He looked down at me. "I'm going to bring you something to drink." He felt my forehead. "She's burning up! How many did they give her at once?"

"They gave her four shots."

"Four! Were they purposefully trying to kill her? I'll be back!" he yelled and stalked out of the room.

My head throbbed, and my body was so tired and weak. I couldn't even will myself to sit up. I remember when I was little, I got into a nest of fire ants. The pain from their bites didn't even compare to the agony I just experienced.

"Luxina, can you hear me?" The voice I didn't recognize was speaking directly to me. "I'm sorry. I'm sorry I said those things. Just hang in there." It had to be Xavier talking to me. I still couldn't answer back. Even the strain of thinking sent fiery ripples through my body. "Grandmother, is she going to be ok? What can we do? She won't make it through another round of those injections."

"I don't know what we can do. We have no way to stop them unless Damian convinces Alpha otherwise." Her voice was faint in my ears. My chest heaved up and down, trying to gulp down fresh air to fill my burning lungs.

There was a commotion in the hall, and two men hovered over top of me again. "You can't give her anymore! You will kill her!" Damian yelled, pushing them away from me. I watched as one of them pinned him to the wall.

"Are you going soft already, Damian? Maybe we should give you your dose sooner. Your angelic blood is fighting it off sooner than last time." The one remained hovering over me, smiling insidiously down at me.

"Leave my sister alone!" Damian yelled, and the other man pulled him out into the hall and shut the door.

The one that remained bent over me. "This will be fun. You're a fighter. Your blood is stronger than what we thought so Alpha said to up the dose."

"Leave her alone, Abaddon!" Lilith yelled.

"Oh, Mother, you cast me out in the darkness and made me this way. I thought you would enjoy my behavior." I felt the sting of another needle and whimpered. "Shh, little one, just let it run its course." He thrust seven more needles into my arm, and the fire took my body over again.

"Please," I managed to croak out. "Please stop." I knew my begging would be futile. I heard the screams of those they tortured with these injections. I knew there was no relief from it.

"Be a good little girl now," he said and left the room. Damian burst back in the door.

"Luxina, stay with me. Fight the darkness!" he yelled into my ear. It was too late, though; the darkness was beginning to swallow me.

"Find my father," I managed to say before I was totally enveloped in the darkness and pain.

Stories from the bible poured into my mind. The fiery abyss of despair described seemed like a cakewalk compared to the fire that blazed through my veins. It makes you wonder how much accuracy was written in Revelation of how those would be treated if they didn't succumb to the God of the Old Testament. How many souls believed they were truly cast into the lake of fire to burn until God decided they had met their doom and washed their souls clean of the livid waters? It wouldn't come to me, the relief of cool waters. I had made my choice, and I was sticking to it. I had defied Alpha. He would make me pay for the defiance. I felt powerless, mortal, and human. I didn't feel like a god or an angel. I couldn't stop this from happening to me.

An eternity of pain is what it was described as. Who could save me? Who would jump in this burning lake of torture to rescue me? The darkness of my unconscious mind dissolved, and I opened my eyes in the lake of fire. I could see it. It was as real as it was described in Revelation. I could feel the boiling water cooking me as if I were food undercooked and not yet done. The tortured screams I heard earlier filled the lake, and I could see their faces, the faces of the damned. Their skin was melting away. And I believed if mine could melt away, some sort of relief would envelop me. Without nerve endings, you can't feel pain!

I turned my face from the lake and saw dragons filling the water with their putrid fire, sustaining the heat in the lake. I watched as creatures filled the lake with gasoline to keep it burning hot and wild. Is that what the lake was? Pure gasoline? I began to choke as I convinced myself I was gulping down gasoline instead of the boiling water. I felt my throat and lungs incinerate. Death at last! But death did not come to me. I sat choking on the fire and gasoline. Each breath I took in felt shorter and shorter, and I assumed I would suffocate as opposed to burning alive. Still, I kicked and thrashed about in the water, sucking more and more of the burning liquid down my throat.

I was locked in this nightmare, the pit of eternal damnation. "You could end this pain," a voice called out in the lake. End the pain? Yes, I want to end the pain. "I just need your blood." What? My blood? No! No! "Then continue to suffer." The fire seemed to grow larger and hotter after the voice left. Had Xavier been tortured this way? If so, how is he still alive? Did they believe me to be weaker than him, more susceptible to giving in? I smiled inwardly. I lived my life in darkness. The dark is my best friend, the only love I know. The dark is what soothes me, the only thing I have ever been accustomed to. I am the light in the dark. I am the candle of freedom that burns bright no matter how fierce the wind blows trying to snuff it out. I am strong. I do not bend. I do not break.

"I will not bow!" I yelled out from the molten lake of lava. "I will not break!" I yelled louder, screaming with what breath was left in my lungs. "You will not make me falter. I will not fall! I am stronger than you are! I am not your child! I am my father's child! I am a firefly!"

The pain lasted and was intense, but I coped with the agony from it. The lake started to dissolve around me, and darkness swept across me once more. The dark was blissful. Through the dark, I saw a light develop. It began to grow brighter and brighter. When I reached the light, my eyes focused on a face.

"We have to get you out of here." Xavier leaned over me, trying to break the manacle shackling me to the bed. I looked over to where he had sat and saw the holes in the wall where he had pulled himself free.

"How..." I whispered breathlessly.

"You are not the only one who is your father's child," he replied. He heard me at the lake. Was he there, too? I didn't see him there. How did he hear me?

The shackle clattered to the floor, and I felt lifted in his arms. "Wait, wait, where are we going? We can't leave grandmother." The words trickled from my tongue.

"There's no time. You need to leave before they kill you," Lilith said. "I will be fine. Go!"

I had no time to argue. I felt the cool rush of wind on my face. I opened my eyes and saw we were in the air. My arms wrapped tighter around

Xavier, who in return, tightened his grip around me. "Where are we going?" I croaked out.

"We're going to Stygia, the only place we will be safe," he replied.

"What about the Glade? My father? That's where he will be..."

"No, they will search the Glade. Whoever stands against Alpha to turn you over will die. We must find power. The Watchers were the strongest angels. They can handle whatever he sends."

"What if they won't help us?"

"They will help us." He sounded so sure of himself.

The frigid air against my skin felt like heaven, but the burning poison coursing through my veins still had me balled up in pain. I began to drift back into the darkness, and the fire returned like a nuclear bomb being dropped on me. I felt myself free-falling through the blackness, and then I thudded.

"Luxina! You must stay awake! You're thrashing about!" I couldn't help but drift off into the void. The burning lake returned, and I could see a figure standing above the fire. The picture of Dante's Inferno doesn't compare to the monstrosity that stood before my eyes. The figure had the head of a bull and the body of a horse. Its tail whipped at me like a lizard tail striking me and tearing the flesh from my body. I howled in pain.

"Do you think you can escape me?" the voice boomed. "Every time you close your eyes, I will be there!"

An icy cold gripped me, and I began choking. The lake vanished, and I pried my eyes open trying to suck in air. My lungs filled with water, and my eyes stung from seawater piercing the tissue. I thrashed in the water, trying to get to the surface to cough the water from my lungs. Hands grabbed me by my waist, and I fought with all my might to be loose from them. They felt hot, unnatural against the cold of the water. Within minutes, I was on the shore of a beach, coughing up the salty water that had infiltrated my lungs.

"Are you ok?" a voice echoed in my ear. I could barely breathe, barely see, and all my senses were distorted. I spit mouthful after mouthful of water out. "Luxina!" the voice shouted. The hot hands returned to my body, and I smacked them away, trying to fight them off. The hands felt like the poison in my veins, burning me from the outside in. "Luxina, stop! It's me!"

My brain started to register everything. I had thrashed around in Xavier's arms, and he lost his grip, dropping me into the ocean. His hands felt unnatural on my skin. "Why are your hands so hot?"

"You're burning up with fever! Your body is registering it as hot, but they're really colder. We have to get you to Stygia." He picked me up in his arms, the torturous heat back on my skin. I expected to feel the cold rush of air, but the wind was seized from my lungs. When I blinked my eyes and reopened them, we were no longer at the ocean but at the entrance of a mountain.

"The Glade," I breathed in relief.

"No, this isn't the Glade. It's the entrance to Stygia, where the Watchers and Nephilim are. Belial should be here." He walked through the cave entrance and deeper into darkness. I fought with all my will to stay awake. I knew what would happen if I drifted off into the black of my mind.

A voice echoed through the passageway of the cave. "Announce yourself and say why you are here. Trespassers are not welcomed too kindly."

"Baphomet, we need to see Belial right away," Xavier replied, struggling to hold me in his arms.

"You know the rules. You must first send for admittance before just showing up. There are rules—"

"Baphomet! Take us to Belial. Alpha has poisoned her blood with demon blood injections. If we don't get the toxins removed, she could die!" Xavier pushed past Baphomet, winding down the dark tunnel. I felt a swift gush of air as Baphomet swooped past us two.

"Follow me. He won't be happy about this."

We were led through tunnels and passageways that zigzagged and winded downward. My ears began to pop, so I knew we were descending faster than the air pressure could keep up. We soon found ourselves in a cavern that was lit by torches. I looked around and saw at least twenty to thirty people standing around. My vision was starting to duck in and out with tiny white spots floating around. There was a rush to my head and a tremendous pain that wrenched me from Xavier's arms.

"Please, someone get Belial!" Xavier shouted as he leaned over me.

"What's wrong with her?" I heard a woman's voice ask.

"Baphomet, you know the rules. They are instituted for a reason," another voice chimed.

"I didn't have a choice, Ozael. He said Alpha had poisoned her blood with demon blood. Watchers or not, rules or not, we are still angels and bound to protect one another!" Baphomet yelled.

I began to convulse again. I could feel my body thrashing and kicking, lashing out at anything close to me. "We have to hurry," Xavier urged. Foam began to pour from my mouth, and my body stiffened.

"How long has she been having the seizures?" another voice echoed through the cavern.

"A day. Damian said they overdosed her with the injections," Xavier replied to the voice.

"How many did they give her?" it asked again.

"Twelve," he replied.

"Belial, is it too late to do anything?" the woman's voice asked again.

"I don't know. We will do everything we can for her, though. She is the daughter of Sophie and Incaendiel," Belial replied. I felt a hand brush my hair and a slight prick in my arm, and I fell out into the dark abyss.

The fire was tolerable this time. It burned, but it was nowhere near the pain I had felt while in the Lake of Fire. I looked down at my searing flesh and saw that the flames were beginning to die down and flicker. My skin's busting, oozing blisters were beginning to diminish in appearance, and my skin was returning its original shade of creamy ivory. Soon, I found myself drifting off into a somber state of darkness. No pain, no agony, just sleep, and sleep I did.

# INCAENDIEL

# CHAPTER 6

"ANY NEWS?" I asked as I walked into the gathering hall. Metatron and Michael stood bent over maps strewn across the table. They looked up with a grimace and shook their heads. I sighed heavily. It had been three weeks since they had taken Luxina. There wasn't a sign of her anywhere. None of those we had captured for information were speaking, either from fear of what Alpha would do or for fear of what I might do when I heard the news. Alpha had disappeared into thin air once more, and we had no leads on his whereabouts aside from the ones we had when we started the hunt.

"Don't give up hope, Incaendiel. News will pop up soon," Michael offered, as I paced back and forth at the table. It was easy for him to say. It wasn't his child that was kidnapped by an insane, tyrannical dictator God. I leaned over a chair and gripped the back of it with my hands. I was beyond irritation or aggravation. I was sinking into a hole I didn't know how to swim in, the hole that I had fought so many times in the past, the dark abyss from which there was no return from.

I felt a hand sweep over my back, and I regained my wits. It was the hand of salvation that has always pulled me from the fathoms of the deep. I looked up into Sophie's eyes and was overwhelmed with emotions.

"Come," she motioned with her head. "Take a walk with me." She started through the doorway, leaving me staring after her.

"Go. As soon as we have news, we will come for you," Metatron said.

I nodded my head and walked from the room, following the weaving trail her light left behind in its wake. I found myself twisting through the corridors and popping out in the throne room

Mother used to take refuge in. I followed the luminescence through the door behind the throne and popped out in the meadow. The one and only time I had been here was with Mother ten years ago.

I found Sophie sitting beneath the tree in the middle of the meadow, watching as the seasons went through their abrupt changes. She sat mesmerized in wonder as she watched the leaves brown and fall, the snow cover the ground, and then the sunshine reappear, melting away at the snow-covered banks.

I sat down beside her and pulled her close to me, wrapping her into my body. We sat in silence, watching the ebb and flow of the seasons before us. "I never imagined this would turn out to be how our existence would unfold," she said. "We have to find them, Incaendiel, but we cannot blame others for the result not being what we want to hear." She always had a way with her words with me.

I turned my attention to the ground where the river cut through. Maneuvering its way from the water was a snake. It didn't move too fast, but it wasn't a hesitant slither as well. I stood from my sitting position and began to walk to the serpent. When we came within a few feet of each other, it stopped moving and stood up as if in a strike position. I went to smack it down, but no sooner had I reached my hand toward it, it had disappeared. I turned to walk back to Sophie, and there it stood in a strike pose behind me. It was taunting me as a cobra would taunt its prey. I picked my foot up to stomp it, and once again, it was gone. I turned in a circle, looking for the creature, when I heard a startled gasp from Sophie.

I spun around to face the tree we had been sitting under, and there, in front of Sophie, taunting her in a strike pose, was the snake. Even though she had let out a startled cry, she looked serene and composed. It looked as if she were staring straight through the snake as if she was hypnotized. It proceeded to curl up her arm when I ran to her, and was about to smack the snake away when she threw up her hand in protest.

"No, Incaendiel. It's Andromalius," Sophie said in a monotonous tone. "He is telling me about the kids." She touched my hand, and I was frozen in place.

"Hello, Incaendiel. I hope I find you well today. I'm here to deliver some good news and some bad news. The good news is that Xavier was able to escape from Alpha with Luxina. The bad news is that Alpha used injections on her, and we are currently pulling the demonic poison from her blood." Andromalius was precise, with no emotions in his voice.

"Injections? What the hell was he doing to my daughter?" I was furious.

"Calm, Incaendiel. We are reversing any and all of its effects. She did the hardest part already by not accepting the injections and rejecting them with her mind. Once we get her stable, we will wait until the coast is clear and then deliver them to you."

"No, there will be no waiting. We will come to her at once." I began to pace in my mind although my body remained still.

"You cannot come here, Incaendiel. It will draw too much attention. This way is better for all of us," Andromalius replied.

"Well, has the group at least considered our proposal to join the Guardians of Light? It will be a war the world has never seen." I wasn't sure of what his answer would be, but there was a slim chance of them joining.

"We will be holding council here in the next few days once we get all the poison out of your daughter's system. Right now, we have seven healers pulling it out, and three of them hold seats on the council. As soon as we come to an answer, I will come in person to deliver our answer. Do not give up hope, Brother. The odds are in your favor as of now."

The snake retreated from Sophie's arm and slithered back to the river, disappearing into the water. I didn't know what to say or how to respond to the information he gave us.

"There was word in Evermore that Alpha had been concocting potions and injections to combine the powers of the wicked he had created." She sat staring where the snake had disappeared into the water. "He experimented on Luxina, but not Xavier…why? Who knows how long that monster has been giving Damian injections?"

"We don't know for sure he has been," I replied, trying to coax her out of her trance.

"Are you seriously trying to say he acted the way he did because he truly loves Alpha?" Her words were bitter and angry. "All you care about is finding your daughter. You don't care about my sons at all, even if one of them is your flesh and blood. You don't care!" She stared at me with hatred in her eyes.

"Oh, you're making this out to be my fault? Whose lover was it that kidnapped one of the kids and helped kidnap the other kid after locking YOU in the tower? Don't turn this on me, Sophie. Every move I ever made was to protect you, to keep you from harm, to keep you from dying! I stood on the edge of the cliff that night and was going to take the plunge. I couldn't bear living without you, and you couldn't stay with me! The darkness would have seeped into you. You weren't strong enough to hold it off. So, I sacrificed us for you to stay alive.

"Just as I was about to slip over, I heard it. I heard her cry. She saved me. She gave me a reason to keep going. She's all I have had for ten years. You have been surrounded by a sea of angels. All I have known has been mortals. I had to hide her growth anomaly and move from place to place. But that doesn't matter to you, does it! All you're worried about is getting *your* sons back. The son you couldn't even bring to meet his father. If you had visited me or sent someone to give me a message, you would have known about your daughter.

"Do *not* try to make me out to be the bad guy in this situation. We are both equally hurt, and we both want our kids back. Right now, we need to stick together and not blame each other." I was harsher than I meant to be, but I believe she got the point.

"Lucifer was right about you. All these years…you have changed." She stood up and made her way from the center of the field to the exit door. I remained behind, sitting beneath the willow.

*Had it truly been too long for us to recover what we had?* I had spent millenniums trying to get her to remember who I was, to remember our love, and was met with obstinance. I finally broke through to her to find out she not only had been having an affair with the same angel who tormented me for years, but also had a son with him. How in all this did I come out to be the bad guy? I sacrificed my love for her to live. I brought her back from the dead, something we are forbidden to attempt.

She was blind to see the extent Alpha had manipulated Damian into being. He was, after all, the one who took Luxina. She wasn't there to see the look on the kid's face. It was pure hatred and evil. It was almost as if he blamed Luxina as if she were a torturing device Alpha used against him. I can only imagine what he was put through by Alpha to turn him into what he is, but it was no excuse for his actions. Lucifer, on the other hand, was just doing what I would have done to get my child back. Even so, what they both did was unforgivable in my eyes.

I sighed and stood up. So much had changed in the last ten years, and there was no end to it still. My life had been unraveled in the blink of an eye, and I made the wrong decision and trusted the wrong person with the other half of my being. I'm sure she hated me for handing her over to Lucifer, but I knew it was the only way for us to survive. She had to go to the Summit. I couldn't let the darkness turn her into what I am. I still don't understand what we were, what we had been crafted into. I have yet to see another angel with our powers.

As I crossed the field, there was a shift in the atmosphere in this field of dreams. Something was off, and I could feel it. I turned back around to face the willow tree in the center of the field. The leaves had begun to change colors, and one by one, they slowly floated to the ground. This I had never witnessed and was fairly sure it wasn't supposed to happen. The breeze stopped blowing, and it felt like time had come to a standstill.

The ground began to tremble beneath my feet. The earth broke open beneath the willow tree, and it caved into the molten core that flowed beneath it. The field started to burn, and smoke filled the area. The skies darkened, and lightning crackled through the air. The last remnants of the tree sank into the magma, catching fire and disappearing. The lava began to overflow onto the hill and slowly trailed down the field, catching every plant on fire.

I ran to the exit of the concave and pushed through the building. I was met with a handful of concerned eyes as I burst through the door.

"Everyone must get out now! The mountain is going down!" I yelled.

We all dispersed, running to the different tunnels and signaling everyone to get out as fast as they could blink. We all made it to the top just as the mountain exploded and erupted into a volcanic plume of fire. I searched frantically up top for Sophie. I began to zig-zag in between all the others.

"Sophie?! Has anyone seen Sophie?!" I yelled frantically.

Everyone stood in silence as the answer came to me. She wasn't here. I turned back to the mountain and walked closer. It felt like a bomb had gone off, and I was caught in the shell shock aftermath. I felt arms on me, and I shrugged them off as I walked closer to the burning mountain. Arms wrapped around me, and I fought them off. I was soon overcome by dozens of arms and pulled to the ground. I heard a frantic yell erupting through the crowd and tried to drag myself closer. I knew it was her scream. *She was in the mountain!*

I hadn't noticed I had been crying until I felt the wetness on my chest. I hadn't known I had been the one screaming until my hearing was restored.

"What the hell happened in there?" Metatron yelled, shaking me. "Did you set the Glade on fire?! You could have killed us all! And now Sophie…" he trailed off as he saw my face. I could only imagine what I looked like at that moment. My heart was tearing in two all over again. For the last time, the final time, I had lost her…forever.

"It wasn't you," Michael stated as he loosened his grip on me. I shook my head. "Then what was it? Are there Alpha's doings?"

I shook my head again. I knew what this meant. I knew deep down what had happened. "It's Mother…" They all dropped their hands off me.

"What do you mean it's Mother?" Samael spat through gritted teeth.

"We were in the concave. Andromalius came to us with news."

"What news did Andromalius have?" Metatron asked.

"They have Xavier and Luxina. Alpha injected her with demon blood, and they were pulling the
174

poison out." I swallowed the lump back in my throat.

"What about joining us as an alliance?" Michael asked.

"They haven't met yet. The healers are the council members. They said give them a few days."

"What does this have to do with Mother?" Samael asked again, more annoyed.

"The willow died in the middle of the field and fell into the core. It set fire to the concave and erupted the entire mountain. The concave was Mother's sanctuary. Something must have happened to her. This mountain is part of her."

Everyone grew silent. "Alpha has her," a voice from the back of the group called out. Everyone turned to see who said it, although Incaendiel already knew who it was.

"How do you know Alpha has her?" Samael asked viciously.

"Do you honestly doubt my visions, Brother?" Gabriel called out as he made his way to the front of the line.

# LUXINA

# CHAPTER 7

I OPENED MY EYES, and blue lights swirled all around me. My vision was still blurry and dimmed in and out. I could still feel the faint touch of fire coursing through my veins. I tried to lift my head and sit up, but it felt like I was tied down. I began to panic.

"She's awake," a voice called out.

"Well, put her back to sleep, Aislinn," another voice replied.

"I don't know if I can, Camael. No one has ever broken my sleep state before," Aislinn replied.

"Well, we need to do something fast. I cannot work on her unless she is completely under," a different voice replied.

"Irisael is right. Her eyes have blood spots in them, which means severe trauma that needs to be healed soon. Sanarael, can you help Aislinn put her back under?" Camael asked.

"I'm no Raphael, but I can try. It may take three of us to do it," Sanarael replied.

"I will help. I can induce a heavier sleep for her." How many people were in this room with me?

"That's perfect, Somniel!" Aislinn exclaimed.

I saw three people surrounding me. I couldn't make out their faces through the blur, but the glow they had around them was spectacular. I saw a rainbow aura, a baby blue aura, and a pale, yellow glow about their bodies. I blinked my eyes rapidly, trying to clear the haze, but with each eye blink, my vision grew darker and darker. Soon, I was in total blackness once more. Instead of it being a calming black as it was before, I felt my chest tighten in panic. I was afraid of this darkness. This was something I had never experienced before.

Dad had always taught me there was nothing to fear about the dark walls, but something about these walls sent panic and fear through me. I fought back with every ounce in me. I felt a hand touch my skin, and it felt like a blowtorch was cutting through my skin. More hands fell over me, and I screamed in my head from the pain.

"What's happening?!" Camael shouted.

"Something's going wrong. Her body is sucking the poison back in instead of pushing it out. I have all my power trained on her, and it's not helping anything!" Irisael yelled.

"Alpha must have her locked in some sort of hallucination. These injections show her what her deepest fears are. Luxina!" Aislinn yelled. "Luxina, whatever it is you see, it's not real. Do not be afraid!"

The darkness grew more tormenting. Fires began to pop up and surround me in this hallowed space of air. The flames licked at my skin, burning me as they had done in the lake of fire. I was never going to get through this. The injections were permanent. I could feel them seeping into my heart and killing my grace. My chest grew tighter, and I couldn't breathe.

"What are you doing here?!" I heard Camael yell.

*Oh no, he found me!* I knew it had to be someone that Alpha sent. They had tracked me here through the connection in my mind. With each tormenting thought that passed through my mind, the fire grew brighter, stronger, and more heated. My blood felt like it was boiling, and I felt that at any moment my entire body would explode.

"We will fill you in later. How long has she been thrashing like this?" the voice asked.

"She just started when we tried to put her back into her sleep state. We can't work on her conscious, and the sleep state is inducing a hallucination from the injections," Aislinn replied.

"Let me help," the voice stated.

"If we add any more healing waves, it could destroy her body," Irisael retorted.

"Then back off and let me do it," the voice replied.

"Do not step into our territory and boss us around," Camael retorted.

"Do you want her to die or live?" the voice boomed. It sent ripples and shivers through my spine.

In the flames, a face began to form. A hand reached out and grabbed me in the flame. The hand burned into my arm, and I howled in pain. The arm yanked me closer to the flames, and I peered through the fire at who had a hold of me. I felt the breath leave my lungs as I stared into eyes that looked like a reflection of mine.

"Mom?" I asked.

"Let Raphael heal her!" Sanarael yelled.

I was sucked from the flames and darkness. The hand that had held tight to my arm was being pulled along with me, still burning into my skin. It wasn't as bad as the eyes that burned into mine. She mouthed words to me, and I struggled to understand what she was saying. I was being pulled further and faster through the hollow black.

"I can't understand you!" I cried out to her.

Just as the light began to approach, words formed in the air. "This is all your fault!" She released her grip on my arm, and I watched as I was sucked away from her. She never took her eyes off me.

I erupted through a cloud of smoke, and light surrounded me. Sunshine as far as the eye could see covered a valley in warmth. It wasn't the cold, burning warmth of the fire. It was peaceful and serene. I felt it fill me on the inside. As hard as I tried, I tried to let it take my anxiety, but those words and her voice chilled me to the bone. She hated me, and I didn't even know why. I had never met her, and she didn't even know about me. Why would she say those things to me?

Sorrow filtered in through the warmth, and I found myself balled on the ground, crying. The one person I wanted to meet, wanted to love, hated me... Why? What had I done that was so terrible she would hate her own daughter?

"Luxina, sweetie, come back to me," a voice echoed through the valley. I knew the voice, and it swelled my heart to hear it. "Come back to me, sweetie."

"Daddy? Daddy! Help me, Daddy! Save me from this perpetual hell! I can't take it anymore! I'm not strong!" I cried and cried.

"Come to me, sweetie. Follow my voice."

I listened to the echo throughout the valley. My eyes fell on a cave at the bottom of the hill from which I stood.

"Follow my voice."

I walked slowly to the cave, hesitant that I would succumb to the darkness.

"Daddy, I'm scared!" I pleaded.

"It's ok. Follow my voice," he replied.

"How do I know it's not a trick?" I cried. My breath heaved in and out in terror.

"Follow your heart, sweetie."

I walked through the cave and found myself lying on a table. I walked over to myself and analyzed my body. My skin had grayed, and there were red blisters all over me. I swallowed the lump that formed in my throat and choked back the sobs. "I'm so scared," I whispered. "What do I do?" I reached out to touch the cold arm that lay on the table.

I bolted upright, gasping for air. Tears blurred out everything around me. I once again felt hands and arms around me, and I fought with all my might. I struck out with my hands, landing blows against the person in front of me. I would not be taken again. I refused to be taken.

"Honey, it's me. It's me!" I heard crying out through the noise. The arms wrapped around me and pulled me in. I breathed in deep, and the smell hit me, the smell of a meadow, of flowers, of sun.

"Daddy?" I cried out. The arms tightened around me, pulling me in closer.

"Yes, baby, it's Daddy," he replied.

I felt the splash of tears on my face. I threw my arms around him and clung to his chest.

"I was so scared," I whispered. "I didn't... I thought... I thought he had me again," I sobbed. "I tried to be brave. I fought him for so long. I didn't want to give in," I cried.

"You did what most could not do, Luxina. You did not bow to him and his torture," he replied, choking on his words.

"Xavier?!" I yelled in panic. "Where is Xavier? Is he ok? Is he safe?" I asked in bewilderment.

"Xavier is fine. He's waiting with the others."

"Mom... where is she? I saw her..." I cried.

"You saw her?" he choked.

"Yes, in the fire. She said... she told me this was all my fault! I don't understand! Why does she blame me? What did I do wrong?" The sobs heaved out.

"We will talk later about that," he replied.

"Incaendiel, we're not sure if all the poison is out of her system. We weren't able to finish the healing process." I looked around for the face of the voice, and my eyes fell on a beautiful woman with long, flowing, blond hair. Her eyes were purple, and a faint glow of yellow rounded her pupils.

"That's the least of our worries right now. With everyone showing up here, Alpha will be alerted, and he will send out his warriors." I looked around for the voice, and my eyes fell on a man. His eyes were piercing blue but with a red glow to the pupils. His hair was black as night. They both had markings on their skin that resembled tattoos. I looked around at everyone in the room and noticed for the first time that all the angels had these markings as well. Everyone but my father and me had them. I couldn't recall them being on Xavier either. What did these markings stand for?

"Can you keep Xavier and Luxina here?" Incaendiel replied.

"Yes, we can shield them, but the rest of you, I'm afraid our shields can't withstand that much angelic power in one place," Belial replied.

I looked up at Dad wild-eyed. "You can't leave me here!" I protested.

"We will come back for you. Right now, it's not safe for any of us to be here." He brushed the hair out of my face.

"Please, Daddy, don't leave me here," I pleaded. I wrapped my arms around him and clung to his side.

"You will be protected here, and it won't be for long. We must make sure all the poison is removed before you leave."

# CHAPTER 8

IT HAD BEEN A DAY since Dad had left us in the care of the Watchers and Nephilim. I paced quietly waiting for him to return for me. They were nice to both Xavier and me and provided the protection they had promised. I replayed over and over in my head the last few things I could recall from my dreams when I was injected with that serum. The one memory of my mother hurt the most. *Why is it my fault?*

I asked myself that over and over, but I couldn't come up with an answer. Xavier thought it was

Alpha playing a ruse. I don't think that. It felt genuinely like my mother. Her anger and her words made my heart hurt. I wanted to know my mother so badly, and now, she is blaming everything that has happened on me.

As we sat waiting through the day, we had someone pay us a visit. I had never met her before, but her eyes were an amazing color of purple.

"Hello, Luxina. It's good to see you up and about doing better," she said, as she walked into the room.

"Thank you," I replied with a smile. "I was out of it when I was brought here, so I don't know anyone's names. Who are you?"

She smiled. "I am Sophia," she replied. "I came to talk to you about what happened when Alpha had you captive."

"Sophia? You were Lucifer's mate, right?" I asked, sitting down.

She nodded grimly. "Yes, I was. I left him not long after the Garden of Eden exile of Adam and Eve. I came here to be with my brothers and sisters that weren't allowed to return to the Summit. I pleaded with Lucifer to join me. He told me no. He had something he had to take care of before he could join me."

I watched her face as she told me her story. I could see the pain in her face when she spoke of him.

"What would you like to know?" I asked.

"Everything," she said, taking a seat beside me.

Xavier joined us from across the room.

"What did he inject into you?" she asked.

"We aren't entirely sure. All we know is it's supposed to be a concoction of demon blood," Xavier replied.

"Did he inject you as well?" Sophia asked Xavier.

He nodded.

"Why didn't you tell me?" I asked.

"It wasn't important," he replied. "I didn't react like you did. The first injection was painful, but the ones that followed were not."

"What did Alpha tell you, if anything, about what you are? What did he call you?" Sophia asked, glancing between Xavier and me.

"He never spoke to me about what we are. All I know is we are like demigods," Xavier replied. Their eyes turned to me. "Did he tell you anything?" Xavier watched me as I dabbled back and forth, deciding whether to answer or not.

"Yes, he said we were called fey," I replied. Sophia laughed heartily.

"He told you that you were fey?" she asked.

"Yes. I asked if it was like faeries, and he said no, that we were what created faeries." Sophia still grinned at the joke, and I had no clue what it was.

"You two are not fey," Sophia chuckled. "Alpha lied to you, Luxina. The fey are broken into two segments: The Light, which are called the Seelie Court, and the Dark, which are called the Unseelie Court. They were created from the Old Gods of Atlantis. They are literally the faeries of the myths, alongside the nymphs and sprites. Those that are of the race were created by an old God that goes by the name of Enki."

"Enki? Like Enkidu from Egyptian lore?" I asked, growing more curious.

"I see they still teach about ancient civilizations among the humans," Sophia smirked. "Yes, that is the same Enki. He frowned on Alpha when he went to Dragonazi for help to create all the 'evils' of the world."

"Why haven't any of the angels ever been told about the others? The other gods? We have always thought it to be Alpha and Omega," Xavier interjected.

"Omega, or Lilith as she goes by now, wanted to clue all the angels in on it. Alpha refused. He believed they would turn their backs on him and take to the other gods and goddesses. He has always been a jealous god, so jealous he thought he needed an adversary."

Sophia paused, flitting her eyes between us.

"I never imagined Incaendiel would have become his true adversary. Lilith never had it in her heart to go against Alpha. However, when she created your parents, when she added the special and extra ingredients, she awakened an incredibly old power. Once I left Lucifer's side and banished myself to Earth, I came to Lilith, my mother, where she confided in me a secret. Even Alpha didn't know about the secret. When they created the angels, all of us, they used their power alone in doing so. When it came to creating Sophie and Incaendiel, she mixed a few ingredients together and molded them within their bodies before they brought them into existence."

"Angels weren't just 'thought' into existence? They were molded like humans?" I asked, confused.

"Yes and no. Humans were molded from the dust of the Earth, where they return when they die.

Angels were molded from the dust of stars," she replied.

"So, what were the ingredients she used in making our parents?" Xavier asked.

"She took the feather of a phoenix to give them power over fire. The Seelie court offered up a bit of their faery dust to create an enchantment."

"What kind of enchantment?" I asked.

"No one knows for sure. Neither of your parents ever dared to venture to the Seelie realms because of how precious they are and would be coveted to keep, especially by Mab," Sophia replied.

"Who is Mab?" I asked.

"The Dark Queen of the Unseelie court," Sophia replied.

"What else did Lilith add to make our parents?" Xavier asked.

"Lilith traveled to the deepest fathoms of the universe and found a star, an old star, the first and largest star to have leapt into existence. This star was a sun in another galaxy where other gods and goddesses ruled over their intelligent creations. These civilizations were dying off as their sun began to fade. The solar system was being abandoned in search of life elsewhere to cohabitate with other life forms."

"Aliens!" I interrupted. I blushed from the outburst.

"Yes, what humans call aliens were these other civilizations. Lilith went to the galaxy before the sun began to supernovae and grow cold to take the power the sun was relinquishing into the universe. She added this power into her moldings and then, alongside Alpha, poured life into them. She had once asked Dragonazi what the oldest creations that existed above gods were. He told her only those born from the power of the universe hold more power and are above the gods. He told her they were called Ntidus Assis, the Shining Ones. Only the wisest of gods knew how to rehabilitate this old form of power. She sought out dozens of the crones and sages until she found her answer and made your parents."

"Who is Dragonazi?" I asked.

"An old, old God that Alpha had sought help from prior to Lilith taking the fall as his adversary," Sophia replied.

"So, he gave her the idea to make our parents? And in turn, their power made us?" I asked. "What else did this power make?"

"The gods used to take this power and add a slight drop to their human creations. This is where

Indigo, Crystal, and Rainbow children come from; they are earthly star children. You two are Stellar Star Children, as well as your parents; always created in a pair to reproduce...twin flames."

I sat back and drank all this in. *Shining Ones? Could it be that was why Alpha feared my dad?*

"Is that why the injections wouldn't take?" I asked. She nodded. "What about Damian? He is half a shining one, right? They must continuously dose him because he burns through it. Is there such a thing as half a star child?"

"I haven't looked into it that far, but Damian is Sophie's son. I would have to consult Dragonazi for a definite answer. What I do know is we need to get Damian away from Alpha as soon as possible before the injections do take. Part angel, part star child with demon blood...that's a scary thought. Who knows how much longer his blood can fight off the injections?"

"Will the Watchers help us? I mean, not just to save Damian, but also to take down Alpha for good. For too long, he has destroyed everything that was dear to me. My parents spent millennia apart; Xavier and I were kept apart for ten years because of him. Now, he has Damian and tortures creatures for their blood to experiment with. He's a monster!"

I hadn't realized how angry I was with Alpha until this very moment, but I truly despised him.

"I will hold council with the others and give you your answer by dawn's first light. It will take more than just us Watches to take him down. If agreed upon, we have a lot of work creating an alliance of fighters against Alpha."

I drank everything in. I sat with everything spinning around in the void of my mind. Dad had always told me how manipulative Alpha was. I rolled everything over in my mind so far that I had been taught.

"Sophia, if you don't mind, I need more information," I said, still staring out into space as I spoke. "My father has always spoken of the evil that Alpha was. He said he used propaganda to insinuate wars on earth, but I need more details than that."

"Are you sure you are ready for this information download?" she asked. "It's a bit more than what most people hear their entire lives." I nodded my head and glanced up to her, locking my eyes on hers. "Very well." She took a deep breath and exhaled. "Humanity has always been preyed on by

Alpha. Lilith really pissed him off when she snaked into the Garden and told Eve to eat the fruit of knowledge. He has worked consistently to not only keep humanity from learning of the Goddess but also so humanity wouldn't know how evil he was."

"I'm sure your father taught you about the Illuminati and the Luminari brotherhoods, correct?" Sophia asked. I shook my head. "Well, I will tell you two different stories of who they are. One story society believes them to be, the other is who they really are. To get to these stories, I must also go into the story of Atlantis. I mentioned Atlantis earlier, but I didn't think of going into the story.

"Before the birth of Lucifer born flesh as Jesus, there existed this place called Atlantis. It was said that their civilizations were powered by a god other than Alpha. A hod older than he and more powerful than he, the God Enki that I told you of. This made Alpha sorely angry. The gods who had created this place of wonder in the world were given permission to do so by Lilith, who had domain over Earth after the fall. The same gods who gifted your parents with their sun's energy are the same ones who created the inhabitants of Atlantis. Many believe that they may have been the actual extra-terrestrials from the solar system abandoned after the sun died.

"These people were beyond any advancements of the humans that lived here on earth. However, their presence sparked creativity in the humans of Earth. The Mayans created the temples and all the structures of their civilization. The Egyptians built their pyramids and other iconic statues. The influence wasn't noticeable at first. With each advancement of nations, Alpha became increasingly jealous. The influence this society had over his creations made him angry. He thought only he should be able to persuade his creations.

"Word got about in the cosmos, and Enki knew Alpha would try to destroy the city of enlightenment. They withdrew the civilization from the world and buried it deep in the depths of the earth. When they withdrew the civilization, the influence that was held over humanity dissipated. This took Earth from the fourth dimension of existence into the third. The power the gods had in this world came to neutrality as they saw that Alpha would do whatever he wished to do.

"Alpha thought he could pull all the free-thinking humans back to his side when he sent Lucifer to the world to walk as Jesus. Lucifer did the opposite. Instead, Lucifer influenced his followers to break farther away from Alpha and closer to the Goddess. Instead of being a poster boy for Shamballa, he fronted Agartha. The two of them together created the Brotherhood of the Snake. Shamballa, being that of the Illuminati, is the Red Dragon, and Agartha, being that of the Luminari, is the Yellow Dragon. This enraged Alpha, so he worked quickly to make amends for it. He made sure the authentic teachings never made it into the minds of man.

"Shamballa, the Illuminati, want a government-controlled world. When the government controls the world with the access point directly connected to religion, world domination is shown. The withdrawal of Atlantis really hurt the ebb and flow of free thinking. However, those connected to the divine oneness of the Dark Mother were able to lift the veil of truth from their eyes. Those that were consciously aware of what the Illuminati were monopolizing from created factions. The Rosicrucians were born and later grew into the Freemasons. They were led strictly by those of the fallen.

"The Illuminati retorted by using the inspiration that Atlantis had on Egypt and exploiting the iconic symbol of the all-seeing eye with the pyramid. They also labeled the Luminaris with that of Alpha's name to confuse the followers who sought the feminine divine. Alpha then labeled the Illuminatis as Omega, even though their energies were masculine. Agartha was clearly seen as solace and sanctuary for the Atlantean priests who were seeded and dispersed. At long last, they took refuge among them before the Illuminati could wipe out the Kumaras for good. Without their influence in the world, there would be absolutely no way around the Illuminati.

"With the rise of the Illuminati, Alpha was able to manipulate and plot against the Dark Mother. With Eve taking a hit by eating from the Tree of Knowledge, women were slowly pushed to the back part of the brain as opposed to being superior to men. They were looked at as taints; they were the cause of their departure from the Garden since submission was lost to them, thanks to Lilith. Women were the reason man was damned. Ultimately, the influence Alpha had over men and how a woman was perceived enabled Alpha to have the priests delete the Dark Mother from existence in the Bible. He then had them perpetuate fear in humans by making the adversary evil and only there to bring down the salvation of man. It was never the plan of Alpha for Jesus to die on the cross. Lucifer was supposed to escape the confines of the soldiers, but he remained behind to be selected to die for his rebellious teachings.

"It has become harder and harder for Alpha to remove the Dark Mother from humanity." Sophia stopped and grew silent.

"So, what you're telling me is that Alpha has personally persuaded lore throughout humanity to destroy grandma from existence in the human world? How did he personally do it? The angels just influenced through touch and thought. Did he literally come down to the humans?"

"Alpha has taken many guises over the years, unbeknownst to the Dark Mother. He has always had his finger dipped into humanity. He would be an advisor to the Presidents of the Nations, or he would be on the council that elects the pope. Anywhere he could possibly influence man to control HIS religion, he was there advising away. The Bible of humanity was written by man but guided by the word of him. He has literally corrupted humanity by instituting the Illuminati and heading it himself."

"So, in order to completely take Alpha down, we would also have to eradicate the Illuminati… right?" Sophia nodded. "What else?"

"We will have to once again embark upon the war that was started millennia ago before Eve was ever brought into existence. We must eradicate any beast or any creature he has made to symbolize the fear that makes humanity cling to religion. We must break down all mythologies, all dogma. We must take out his foundation for existence to weaken him and make him vulnerable. Do you understand what that means?"

I nodded. "We're going to need reinforcements. We will need every fallen angel that was returned to the Summit, all angels willing to fight against him, and more," I said, gazing at her. Our eyes locked, and I could feel the information exchange between our silent minds. "Do you think both the Seelie and Unseelie courts will help us?"

"We will see, Luxina. Right now, we all need our rest. In the morning, the council meets and will decide the point of action.

# CHAPTER 9

MORNING ARRIVED as I waited impatiently for Sophia to bring us news of what the council had said. I had odd flashbacks from my time with Alpha and the lake of fire he had thrown me in. *Why did he need me so badly?* I shook my head and cleared my thoughts when they landed on Damian. I could vaguely remember him leaning over me and asking me if I was ok. Xavier stood beside him, arguing for him to stay away. I could see the frantic look in Damian's eyes. He knew what it felt like. He had been tested on the same way and didn't like it. He helped Xavier escape with me…

"A penny for your thoughts," Xavier murmured, breaking my concentration.

I smiled weakly. "I was just thinking of Damian."

His face fell a bit. "Oh," he replied.

"We need to save him, Xavier. He is our half-brother. He doesn't deserve the treatment he has received from Alpha. He was forced through what we were as well. We have to..." I paused as Sophia entered the room.

We both abruptly stood in her presence.

"News from the council?" Xavier asked.

She stood solemnly. "Yes, but you aren't going to like it."

"Tell us," I implored.

"The Council agreed to join the cause on one condition," she stated, pausing for a moment. She looked between us and sighed. "They will only join in if both the Seelie and Unseelie courts agree to fight in league with us. If either oppose, then we will not be joining the rest of the Guardians to fight against Alpha."

"Well, that's good news!" I exclaimed.

"No, it isn't," Xavier sighed. "The Seelie court hardly lets any creature in that isn't pure fey blood. It would take a great amount of bartering with them."

"Well, what about the Unseelie court?" I asked.

"Oh, they would love to have us there," he replied. "But it's like the Hotel California. You can check out anytime, but you will never ever leave unless they allow you to."

"Xavier is right," Sophia stated. "And between the two of you, they would never let you leave because of how special you are."

"Why?" I asked.

"Because you are a beautiful creature that they don't possess in their realm," she replied.

"Well, it's a chance we are going to have to take," I blurted.

"Absolutely not!" a voice yelled out.

I sighed heavily. "Dad! We can do this!"

He wrapped his arms around me. "I just got you back from that twisted monster. I won't let you walk into a den of even more devious creatures than that of Alpha. I will go," he replied.

"Incaendiel, you mustn't," Sophia argued. "They would keep you as well!"

"They could try. I have had my fair share of dealings with the Unseelies for centuries. They know me and would listen to me. However, the kids are new specimens. They would want to keep them," Dad replied. "But, before anyone goes on any adventure, there are more important tasks at hand that must be seen through."

"Like what?" I asked.

"Like spending time with you and the son I had no clue I had," he replied, looking over at Xavier.

Xavier's face clouded over. "This is more important than catching up. Grandmother was left with that insane lunatic!"

"Mother can hold her own," Dad replied. "I need this."

"There is a chamber off to the right down the hall where you all can spend some catching up time together uninterrupted," Sophia said. "I am going to tell the council the decision was made to implore the fey for help."

Xavier, Dad, and I walked to the chamber that Sophia had directed us to. Xavier took a seat in the corner while Dad and I sat down beside each other. He looked as if he hadn't slept in weeks. It dawned on me...

"How long have I been gone?" I asked.

"Two weeks," he replied.

"What?!" I exclaimed. "Two weeks? It felt like just a couple of days!"

"That's how Alpha manipulates you. He puts you in that room, and you have no sense of reality," Xavier replied.

Dad looked over at Xavier. "I'm sorry."

"For what?" Xavier asked.

"For not being there for you. For not being there to save you. For not knowing you ever existed when, of course, you existed. There are grudges being held for not being told about you that I must deal with myself, but I am sorry no one ever told you about me. I am sorry they never let you see me. It's my fault," Dad replied.

"How is it your fault?" Xavier asked smugly.

"Because I am dangerous to you. Just like I was dangerous to your mother. I have… darkness in me that will never leave. That darkness will harm anything that is bright around me. Once this whole war is over and Alpha is defeated, I plan to send Luxina to stay in the Summit," Dad said.

"What?! No! I am not going anywhere without you!" I replied defiantly. "I am fine! My light is fine! You are not blanching me, Dad! I refuse to go," I said matter of fact. "Refuse."

"Where is my mother?" Xavier asked. "They locked her in the tower was the last I saw of her."

"When we were at the Glade, there was a fire. The entire mountain was destroyed by Alpha's hellfire. I don't know if she just didn't make it out or if Alpha has her. If what Luxina saw while she was out of it is true, then Alpha has her… and he is running experiments on her as well."

"We have to go back!" Xavier yelled, jumping from his seat.

"Where you two were is a fortress!" Dad yelled back. "No way in and no way out! You were lucky once. I am not risking your lives to take you back to save people. That is what the council and the fey are for."

"You can't tell me what I can and can't do, *father*," Xavier sneered.

"Enough!" I exclaimed. "Xavier, listen to Dad. Dad, stop being bossy. We are going to get everyone back! But we must have a plan, like Dad said. We can't run back into a trap."

"Whatever," Xavier replied, storming out of the room.

Dad went to follow, but I stopped him. "Let me. He will listen to me," I said.

Dad gazed at me and smiled. "Just like your mother."

I left Dad behind in the room as I went to look for Xavier. I found him looking at maps in a large library.

"What are you doing?" I asked.

"Looking for where we were so I can go back," he said, walking over to another map.

I followed him and lightly touched his hand. Shock waves of energy ran through me, and I nearly toppled from the surge. He caught me as I was about to fall. I laid into his chest and peered up at him as the energy between us intensified.

"Please, don't leave my side," I whispered.

I saw his face crumple as he leaned in for a kiss and whispered. "Never, my firefly."

Alarms sounded all around us. "Oh no," I breathed. "They're here."

"Take the children to the river, now!" Sophia barked as she ran through the room.

Five Watchers surrounded us and led us out of the room through dark passages and corridors. Before long, we were locked inside a room and were being guarded.

"What's happening?" I demanded. "Where is my father?!"

"When it is safe, we will let you leave. For now, just make yourselves comfortable," one of them replied.

He looked different than Sophia. His skin color was different. "Why don't you look like the other Watchers?" I asked.

"Because we are the Nephilim. We are the offspring of those who were cast out from the wars. The Watchers protect us as they always have. Our parents are both angel and mortal," he replied. "We are the abominations Alpha tried ridding the world of. When the council pledges the allegiance of the Watchers, we pledge our allegiance to our forefathers as well and join them."

I sat thinking quietly to myself when it dawned on me. "Xavier, hey," I said, nudging him. "We can get into the Seelie court."

"What?" he asked, trying to follow.

"Sophia said that Lilith went to the Seelie court for enchantments to make Mom and Dad. We have a touch of Seelie running through our blood. They would let us in," I whispered.

"You heard Dad. Neither of us is going. He is," he replied.

A knock sounded on the door. The Nephilim guards took out their weapons and stood in front of us to protect us.

"It's Sophia, let me in!" she yelled.

They unlocked the door and opened it. Sophia ran in and yelled, "Close it back!"

She had a look of bewilderment on her face.

"Where is my dad?" I asked, standing from my seat.

She looked at me sympathetically. "They took him. Alpha took him. They were looking for you. Lucifer…" she trailed off. "We must get you out of here. The river is just through the back gates," she said, walking to the middle of the floor.

She removed the carpet that laid on top of a door.

"Follow this passage until it ends. Take a boat across the River of pu and get to the Seelie and

Unseelie royalties. Tell them what is happening. Plead with them, beg with them, offer them riches, but do not offer anything of yourself to them. They will try and trick you; they will try to make you stay in their courts." She motioned for the Nephilim I had been speaking with to walk over. "Go with them, Praeziel. Protect them with all your will. They will need it."

She didn't give us a chance to protest. She pushed both Xavier and me through the hidden trap door. Praeziel followed, and she shut it back. We heard the lock locking it in place, and the little bit of light that came through the boards disappeared as she laid the carpet back over top of it. We heard a loud bang as the door burst open to the room we were in.

"Where are they, Sophia?" Lucifer demanded.

"You will never find them, love," she replied.

"Oh, but you are mistaken, dear Sophia," Alpha said.

"Let the other child go, Alpha. You are going to kill him with your experiments," she hissed.

"Oh, I beg to differ. It seems as if the last injection has held out far longer than any other I have given him. Pretty soon, I will make a permanent one and bend you all to my will!" he exclaimed.

*Damian! We are too late to save him.*

"Damian, come here, son," Lucifer called.

"Yes, Lucifer," Damian replied.

"Kill everyone in this room, especially her," Lucifer spat.

"Let's go look for the other two," Alpha said. "They can't have gotten far."

There was silence as everyone left the room.

"Damian, you don't have to listen to them. You don't have to do this!" Sophia pleaded.

"Scream," he said.

# CHAPTER 10

"WE HAVE TO GO BACK and help her!" I protested as Praeziel and Xavier pulled me along in the tunnel.

"We have to do what Sophia said," Praeziel replied.

"We have to help—"

"No! I will not disobey orders from my mother!" Praeziel yelled.

I went silent and stared at him in disbelief.

"Yes, Sophia is my mother. My father wanted nothing to do with me after I was born. He tried to sacrifice me, and she intervened. Alpha had told him to do away with the filthy Nephilim, and she saved me. So, as much as I would love to save her right now, she left me with one final wish. To keep you two safe and make sure you got to the Seelie and Unseelie Queens to pray for help."

"Which one are we going to first?" I asked.

"The Seelie court, of course. We will ask King Oberon and Queen Titania for their allegiance and then follow up with the Unseelie court if Alpha hasn't already beat us to it," Praeziel replied.

"Are they nice?" I asked as we trudged along in the dark.

"The Seelie court caters to humanity. They are the light to the dark," Praeziel replied.

"How do we get there?" I asked.

We reached the end of the tunnel, where the mouth opened to a river that had a boat.

"Everyone, climb on," Praeziel ordered.

Xavier and I climbed on while he pushed the boat and jumped on as it left the dock.

"We must find a meadow of white ash trees. They are the portal into the Seelie realm," he replied.

"In school, we studied Robert Frost. The teacher told us that the largest meadow of white ash trees was in Isle of Mann," I stated.

"Then that is where we have to go," Praeziel replied.

The water forked off into three sections, each of

which was an assorted color stream. There was an ocean blue stream to the left, a black stream down the middle, and a golden stream to the right.

"Do you know which one to take?" Xavier asked as we grew closer.

"Of course," Praeziel replied. "The one down the middle leads you to the mortal underworld. As you know, when mortals die, they do not go to the Summit. The one to the right is a special river that leads you to the Garden of Eden. Our cave was built right where Adam and Eve left the Garden once they were banished. The river to the left is our passageway out of here."

At the mouth of the river stood two large beings dressed in black robes, holding scythes. They crossed the scythes, and the boat stopped.

"Who dares to enter the mortal realm from this entrance?" one of them asked.

"It is I, Praeziel, sent by Sophia herself to serve and protect the Ntidus Assis in their journey to the Seelie courts. We had to take this path since the conclave was under attack," Praeziel stated boldly.

"Passage granted," the other one said.

They lifted their scythes, and the water started flowing once more. The boat lurched forward, and Praeziel bowed to the two figures as we passed through the gates to the mortal world.

Once we were out of earshot, Praeziel said, "Lucky for us, Alpha doesn't have complete control over everything in this universe."

"How does he not have control over them?" Xavier asked.

"They are older than Alpha. They are Guardians of Death. They govern what Alpha cannot touch. He cannot interfere with humanity's souls. Even he is limited in power," Praeziel replied.

We drifted in silence for a while. The scenery was gorgeous as we entered the mortal world. It was nearly technicolor like the Summit was supposed to be. My mind began to stray, and I couldn't help but think of Damian.

"Praeziel?" I asked.

"Yes, Luxina," he replied.

"Will you help me save my brother?" I asked. "He is being forced to do what Alpha wants him to do. He doesn't do it out of free will. Alpha controls him with the same injections that they gave me. We must rescue him from Alpha and detox him the same way I was detoxed before it becomes too late to save him. I don't want to lose him to darkness. This darkness… it isn't like the darkness my father has. It's malevolent like those that are Forsaken but worse."

"The reason it is different from that of your accustomed darkness or even that of Forsaken is because it isn't angelic at all. Omega, your grandmother, requested from the Seelie Queen,

Titania, an enchantment for her elixir to make your parents. Well, we have been doing surveillance on Alpha for a while. He too went to the fey, but not Queen Titania or even King Oberon. He requested court with the Unseelie Queen Mab.

"At first, she refused his request. She didn't want to have any part in the destruction of the natural order of the oldest universal power." He nodded to both Xavier and me. "When she didn't give him what he wanted, he began to kidnap Unseelie fey and drained them of their blood. However, the blood wasn't sufficient on its own. So, he went through them one by one, draining the Unseelies of life. The Queen of Air and Darkness couldn't bear to see her beautiful court dropping like wildflowers starved of water. So, she granted him his request. She withdrew one pint of her own blood for him to use.

"However, there was a price for him to pay as well. If he were to fail with the amount of blood she gave him, he was to never return to the Otherworld. He had to remain a prisoner of the Unseelie court for the rest of his days. There would be no more blood offered than the pint she gave him as well."

"So, he traded his freedom, his godly powers, to create a serum to mutate us into monsters?" I asked flabbergasted.

Praeziel nodded. "And he is close to perfecting

it. Your brother doesn't have much time left before the injections don't burn through his blood anymore. When the injections stop burning, that means they are working."

"What if the injections only burned once? What if they only initially burned, and you didn't feel anything for the rest of them?" Xavier asked.

"Then that means they were successful," Praeziel replied, narrowing his eyes at Xavier. "Why?"

"When he gave me the injections, the first one hurt, but I was so angered by the second injection, I felt nothing. I don't feel any different, though... so are you sure it means they worked?" Xavier asked.

"You may be different. You are full blooded Ntidus Assis. The injection might not work on either of you at all. Your brother, however, is not full blooded. He is a half-blood. So, he is in more danger than either of you ever will be," Praeziel replied.

"How would we know it did work on us?" Xavier asked, with a hint of fear in his voice.

"If it did work, we will soon find out at the Seelie court. They detect anything in your blood that is malevolent," Praeziel replied, with a tad of worry on his face.

"What?" I asked. "Why that look?"

"They may put a kill order on him if he does

have demonic blood in his veins. He poses a threat to their realm," Praeziel replied. "They make you swim in a lake of purity. If the water stays the same, your blood is clean and pure. If it turns black, it means your blood is tainted."

"So, what does that mean?? We were both injected with the serum," I asked.

"Yours was burned out of your blood. Him," Praeziel nodded toward Xavier, "I'm not so sure if it was or not."

"Is there a way we can test that theory? How would we know he still has the serum in his blood?" I asked.

"Not all Nephilim live at the conclave. Some live very mundane lives. I would have to put in an urgent call to a brother who works in a laboratory in a hospital. He would be able to view the malformities under a microscope," Praeziel replied.

"Alright then, first stop is mundane city," I stated.

"There is another way," Praeziel said. "But it isn't a pleasant one; however, it wouldn't involve interrupting the mundane life that the Nephilim lived."

"What is it?" I asked impatiently.

"There is an oracle that lives as a hermit. She is powerful beyond her years. We have protected her entire lineage, which dates back to what is referred to as biblical times. She can sense the presence of angels, demons, and alike. However, we haven't called on her family in years. She may not even know about the war at all. It's a risky chance," Praeziel replied.

"What's her name?" I asked.

"She goes by Starfire," he replied.

Our boat crested a bank, and we all disembarked into a meadow. I had spent my entire life living in the mundane world and never took the time to appreciate my surroundings. I stopped and smelled the flowers and watched the bees buzz. As we walked, the area started to become remarkably familiar. I looked over at Xavier, and he had a wide-eyed look of surprise. I followed his gaze, and in the middle of the field stood a burned tree. I knew that tree.

"Where are we?" I asked nervously.

Praeziel smiled. "I see you two recognize the field. That must mean you have dreamt of this place. This is one of the few holy places on earth. Not many, including angels, know about its location or even what it is called."

I looked around and noticed there were graves far off in the distance. I never remembered seeing them while meeting Xavier here.

"What is this place called?" I asked.

"פוטר של שדה," Praeziel said in Hebrew. "Potter's

Field. This is where the bodies of angels are buried."

I ran toward the graves. I had to see for myself. I crested the top of a field and gasped. There were miles and miles of graves to be seen.

"All these angels were..." I couldn't finish the statement.

"Yes, they were all killed during the war. Their spirits departed to the burial in the sky, Akashar, similar to that of Valhalla," he replied. "We must get a move on. We have a ways to go before we get to where Starfire lives."

We began to walk by the graves that were unmarked. My soul cried out for each and every single angel that had risked their lives on either side for a cause from greed and vanity.

"Does anyone know who is buried here?" I asked.

"In the Summit, there is a room that lists every angel that has died in battle and gone to Akashar," Xavier replied. "I have, um, sneaked in there a few times out of curiosity."

We walked quietly and solemnly past the graves. I couldn't believe the numbers that had been buried. We were always told that there was an infinite number of angels, and it looked like hundreds of thousands had been buried here. I glanced over at Xavier, who was watching my face, and I could see it bothered him how upset I was over this.

"Why don't we just fly there?" Xavier asked, interrupting the silence.

"Several reasons," Praeziel replied. "One: When you're in angel form, you can be tracked. Two: Since you can be tracked and not cloaked, you put her at risk of being killed, which is not what we want at all. Three: I can't fly. Half mortal, remember?"

"Have you ever lived among the mundanes?" I asked.

"When I was of age to take care of myself, Mother granted me permission to live a normal life in the city like other Nephilim," Praeziel began. "I had lived so long in the conclave that being around those who weren't Watchers or other abandoned Nephilim felt… wrong. I often had panic attacks. I hated the train that ran above my apartment. The crowds gave me anxiety. I had to limit what I could say to people. Mundanes aren't supposed to know anything about our world other than their religious beliefs. I returned home about a year after living among humanity. I didn't belong with them nor conformed like my brothers and sisters have."

"My mundane great-grandmother knew, though," I stated. "She was the one who told my mother about all this."

"That was because she was part of the lineage

that Sophie had been reborn in over and over," Praeziel replied. "There are certain humans who are personally clued in on everything by us. There are some that figure everything out on their own, kind of like Starfire. The rest, they are clueless to the war and mindless drones that listen to the teachings that Alpha has plastered across the world through the Illuminati."

We reached the end of Potter's field, and the sun began to set. I took one final look behind me at all the graves we passed and said a little prayer for their souls. So many had died fighting this stupid war. *How could Alpha subject his creations to this type of finality?*

"We will make camp here and start our journey in the morning," Praeziel said. "Unlike you two, I need sleep as opposed to having it as a luxurious passing of time."

\* \* \*

PRAEZIEL LAY SLEEPING while Xavier and I sat up, unable to sleep. We were only able to think about what we had to do.

"It's getting chilly out," I remarked as my breath began forming crystals in the air.

"Yea, it's unusual," Xavier replied, narrowing

his eyes and looking at our surroundings.

Before we knew it, we were ambushed by a bunch of figures in cloaks. They restrained us all, and one stepped forth and removed its hood from its head.

"Gwynevere," Praeziel shouted. "What do you think you are doing? I am on a mission. I am with these two to protect them to get to Starfire, and then from there, we must go to the Seelie court. What do you want from us?" he asked.

"That's exactly what I want with you. See, the Dark Queen has heard about your little travels and wants to meet with you before you see Titania and Oberon. We figured you wouldn't come along without protesting, so we thought we would take you along to see her ourselves," Gwynevere replied.

The troop walked us to a moonless part of the forest. Nightshade shrubs created a path that split through the forest. Misshaped trees grew along the tops of the shrubs. As we walked forward, the atmosphere began to change around us. I could feel an energy buzz as we crossed dimensions. Cypress trees and tall sycamores set a path to the Unseelie Queen's castle.

"I thought unless we were bearing gifts, we wouldn't be allowed in?" I whispered to Praeziel.

"This is different than you requesting court with the Dark Queen," Gwynevere replied. "You were invited."

Weeping Willows stood in front of the castle, and their tree limbs peeled back as we entered through the gate of the Dark Queen. When we entered the castle, festivities were commenced. The castle was lavish in food and drink. All the Unseelie fey were merry with laughter. However, we didn't stop in the common room.

"The Dark Queen wants to hold court with you in her throne room," Gwynevere informed.

We took stairs up a tower and entered the courtyard where the Dark Queen sat upon her throne. She was gorgeous to the eye. She had dark burgundy hair and racy blue eyes. Her skin was fair with dark red lipstick. Her nails had been groomed into talons. Her dress was magnificent, wrapping her in just the right spots. It shone luminescent under the fire glow in the throne room.

"I thought she was supposed to be a hideous dragon?" Xavier whispered to Praeziel.

"Well, when I have noble-blooded visitors, I like to dress down for them," the Dark Queen replied.

"Apologies, Dark One," Praeziel said, bowing. "They are not accustomed to etiquette outside of what they have been taught."

"Ah, but you have young Nephilim. Tell me, how is your dear mother Sophia these days? I haven't seen her since, well, since Christ hung on the cross," she mused.

"I wish I could tell you the truth, Dark One, but the truth is I do not know. When we left the conclave, it was under ambush by Alpha and his men. I fear my mother did not make it," Praeziel replied.

"Do not fret, young one. Your mother is fine," the Dark Queen replied, winking. "Now, as for you two... down to business, young Shining Ones."

"What do we owe the honor of your courtship?" I asked, bowing.

"Smart girl," she replied. "I wanted to meet the children of Incaendiel and Sophie. I did offer up some of my own power in their creation, so it was only right that I get to witness the power of their offspring."

"You offered up your dark gifts to my father's power, didn't you?" I asked.

She nodded. "The twin flames had to be balanced. Titania and Oberon offered their light gifts to Sophie, and I offered my dark gifts to Incaendiel. But with darkness came absolute power. He is stronger and ultimately indestructible as opposed to Sophie," the Dark Queen stated. "One of my most prized possessions, I'm afraid." She smiled. "I would have kidnapped him long ago, but the world needs him. My greed has its limits."

"So, all you wanted was to meet us?" Xavier asked.

The Dark Queen nodded.

"Ok, we met, so we will be on our way," I said.

"No," the Dark Queen replied, looking over Xavier, mesmerized. "He's a delectable little creature, and he will do just fine as a trophy in my gallery of exotic blooded creations. He bears his father's powers and is mine to keep."

"Over my dead body," I shouted, heated with a twinge of jealousy. I walked towards her with flames bursting from my hands. I hardly ever used my powers since we lived among humans, but they were as strong as they ever could be as

I protested protecting Xavier from the Dark Queen.

"On second thought," she said. "You will make a fine addition yourself. Guards, take them both captive," the Dark Queen announced.

"You can't do this!" I shouted. "We are protected by Seelie enchantments! It runs through our blood."

"I can do whatever I want," the Dark Queen replied. "I helped make you; thereby, I own you."

"Alpha will destroy us all unless we stop him. He doesn't care about any creature in the universe. He is bringing about the apocalypse. He is making an army undefeatable. He has enslaved every type of creature there is to make this serum, including Seelies like yourself," I protested.

The Dark Queen nodded. "Why do you think I have taken you captive? I intend to offer you two to him as part of a negotiation. If I offer you up to him, the bargain is he will stop slaying Seelies while performing lab experiments for his serum."

"Don't you get it, though? It's not just about us. He is creating an army for a larger reason, a larger spectrum on the scale. Earth is just a pawn for him. When the apocalypse is over and gone, he's got bigger fish to fry. Think about that! You will be the cause of the destruction of the entire universe, including yourselves! Our side is the side that you need to be on." I was irate.

The Dark Queen frowned as she pondered over everything I had said. "I will make a bargain with you. I have but one request. I want a present. Bring me my present, and you can have your freedom. You fail at bringing me my present, and I will enslave you and turn you over to Alpha," the Dark Queen replied.

"What do you want?" I asked.

"I want the Garden of Eden. We created it, and we want it back," the Dark Queen replied.

"I don't have the authority to just give you the Garden of Eden. I would have to speak to Lilith. She is the guardian over its threshold," I replied.

"You need not worry about Lilith anymore. Lilith is not on your side," the Unseelie Queen remarked with a dry smile.

"What does that even mean?" Xavier asked.

"It means that she has joined forces with Alpha once more," the Dark Queen laughed.

"I don't believe you. No, Grandmother would

never do that to us. She would never trade off her children. She loves us too dearly to do so," Xavier replied.

"It is true. Fey cannot lie and have no intention of doing so. However, they never tell you the whole truth so they can sway you with their own truths," Praeziel replied.

"The boy speaks the truth. No Fey, whether Seelie or Unseelie, can speak mistruths. We may be benevolent and mischievous, but we cannot lie. Therefore, it lies solely between you two. Would you give up the Garden of Eden to save yourselves and the universe? Or would you refuse me my gift and bring about the turn of the apocalypse?" The Dark Queen asked, grinning.

"What if we were to make this deal with you, and it is the same deal that the Seelie court wishes to make for them to join alliance with us?" I asked.

"I will add additional terms to the bargain. If you are to give the Fey the Garden of Eden back, it will be for both courts of fey. Neither side will have any say over it more than the other side. It will be fair share," she stated.

"Grant us to leave to speak with the Seelie Court, and once we speak with them, we will give you an answer," Praeziel requested.

"You have three days, Praeziel. And then dear Gwynevere will be coming for you again," she grinned wickedly. "I have one more request," she said before we walked through the throne room.

"Yes?" Praeziel asked.

"Your brother Damian," she started. "You must kill him if the serum adheres to his blood."

"Why?" I asked.

"Alpha would be my prisoner then, for there wouldn't be evidence of his success," she replied. "He doesn't know that it bonded with Xavier nor that it bonded with you because you act differently than Damian."

"Wait, what?" I asked, surprised. "It has bonded with us both?"

She nodded her head. "Your blood has extracted the benefits of the serum and rejected all the negative anomalies. However, your brother Damian isn't a full-blooded Shining One. His blood is more susceptible than yours. Unless you save him soon, he will be a lost cause," she replied.

"We need to go then," I said boldly.

I began to walk to the exit when two Unseelie

guards blocked my path.

"What now?" Xavier asked.

"We aren't just letting you go so you can skip out on my agreement," the Dark Queen replied. "I will be sending one of my own with you."

The Dark Queen motioned, and the one named Gwynevere stepped forward.

"Go with them to the Seelie court and ensure their safety," the Dark Queen said. "Make sure Oberon hears them out for this task as well. He can be problematic."

"Yes, ma' lady," Gwynevere replied, bowing.

"Now, you may leave," the Dark Queen stated.

As we left the castle, Gwynevere led us down a path we didn't take to the castle.

"Where are we going?" Xavier asked.

"Seelies have portals throughout their realms that can jump them from place to place. She will be taking us to the gates of the Seelie court through her realm," Praeziel replied.

"Well, at least we don't have to get Starfire involved now, and her protection will be unbroken," Xavier stated.

Praeziel grimaced and looked at Gwynevere.

"You haven't told them!?" she asked.

"I told them what they needed to know to get them there," he replied.

"Wait, what?" I asked. "What are you two babbling about?"

Praeziel sighed. "Your powers are not activated yet. You haven't been trained. Starfire is your trainer. Your parents were never trained. They have untapped potential, even as deadly as they already are."

"Wait, so how can she train us?" Xavier asked.

"Your Seelie enchantments must be activated. There is a reason her name is Starfire. She holds the power to unlock the gifts the universe gave to you. All you lack is the starfire activation. You have the power of the sun resting in your bodies. She can bring it forth," Praeziel replied.

"What could we possibly do with that?" Xavier asked.

"No one knows. You have been a myth until Sophie and Incaendiel came into existence," Gwynevere replied.

"Wait, what about Damian? He is a half Shining One. Can Alpha activate that part of him after the demon blood adheres to his blood?" I asked.

"We don't know," Praeziel replied.

"When we were being held captive, and Luxina was rejecting the injections, Damian was concerned for her," Xavier said. "He only acted like he hated us when others were around until they gave her four doses. It's all been an act. Could it be possible that his Shining blood is doing what ours is doing, and Alpha doesn't know?"

"Yes and no. If Alpha gives him the wrong injection, it can turn him completely demonic. Since he doesn't know about the blood bond, he keeps changing the serum up," Gwynevere replied. "He has to report daily to the Dark Queen."

"What does she really look like?" I asked. "I know it was a façade of what she looked like to us."

"She is a dragon. One of the oldest in creation. One that no one was able to take down. Oberon helped her disguise herself by giving her Seelie blood. This is how we know it does work. She was created from Seelie enchantments and became ruler over all things dark and unnatural," Gwynevere stated.

"Then all the Unseelies... where do they come

from?" Xavier asked.

"The same place Nephilim came from," Praeziel replied. "Mortal bloodlines."

"So Seelies took on human mates?" Xavier asked.

Both Gwynevere and Praeziel nodded.

"We are here," Gwynevere stated.

I looked around, surprised.

"We didn't travel long," I replied.

"We walked through several portals, but you were distracted talking," Gwynevere giggled. "You ready? This leads us to the Isle of Mann. From there, we go through the Seelie portal to the castle."

"We're ready," I replied.

# CHAPTER 11

WE DISEMBARKED the portal at the Isle of Mann. Gwynevere walked us over to a row of white ash trees that lined a path.

"There is the entrance," she said, pointing straight down the path.

"Aren't you coming with us?" Praeziel asked.

"No," she said, shaking her head. "Unseelies like me are shunned from the court. The king could have me locked up for even breaching the gates."

"Yes, he can," a voice shouted.

We looked back to the path we were supposed to take, and a manly creature stood there. I could only assume he was a Seelie.

"Ramon," Gwynevere stated. "What do we owe the pleasure for you greeting us outside of the portal?"

"King Oberon and Queen Titania learned of your journey here and requested we meet the lot of you here and bring you in personally," Ramon replied.

"Another escort," I replied, rolling my eyes. "Fine, we will come along."

"We will see you when we are done speaking with the court nobles," Praeziel said to Gwynevere.

"No," Ramon stated. "She comes too."

Gwynevere's face turned fearful.

"I must have your word that she is to remain unharmed and released at the end of this meeting, or she does not come with us," I said.

"I cannot guarantee any of that. I do not have the authority," Ramon replied.

"No, it's ok. I will go," Gwynevere stated.

"You don't have to risk your life," Praeziel replied quietly.

"I have to do this, love," she said, brushing his face with her hand.

"That explains a lot," Xavier whispered in my ear as we crossed the threshold into the Seelie realm.

.

* * *

"YOUR MAJESTY, here are the travelers as you requested," Ramon said as he led us into the noble's hall.

"Excellent, Ramon. Good evening, travelers. How may I help you?" King Oberon asked.

He had a pinkish hue to his skin and was much, much younger than I imagined him to be. Queen Titania sat silently to his left and watched on. She was a beauty! She reminded me of the Dark Queen, except all her colors were pastels.

"We have come to ask the Seelie court to stand alongside the Watchers, the Nephilim, and the angels of the Summit as we battle Alpha in his apocalyptic war," I replied.

King Oberon laughed. "You want us to join forces against Alpha? We have no quarrel with Alpha."

"He has slaughtered numerous Seelies, and you say you have no quarrel with him?" Gwynevere objected.

"Quiet, half-breed. I don't even know why I told them to allow you in court. Guards, take her outside of the castle," Oberon ordered.

"Is that the way you treat your subjects?" I asked. "How are you considered the light and Queen Mab the Dark Queen? Your duty is to protect humans. Humanity needs you before Alpha sets the apocalypse into motion. Are you going to let your loyalty to Alpha outweigh the needs of the world, including your own?"

"The Seelie realm exists out of space and time. Whatever Alpha does, he does to his own timeline, not ours," Oberon replied cheekily. "So, I will do whatever I want."

"Let's go, Luxina. At least we can still hold up our end of the bargain with the Dark Queen and give her the Garden," Xavier replied.

Oberon abruptly stopped laughing. "The garden?" he asked. "What garden?"

"The Garden of Eden. We are exchanging it with the Dark Queen for our freedom. She has agreed to cooperate with us, unlike you," I replied.

"Out of the question. She does not deserve the garden. Give it to me," he demanded.

"No. Bargain is the Garden will belong to all the fey whether they be Seelie or Unseelie, full breed or half-breed," I replied.

"I forbid it. We created the Garden—"

"And you gave it away. We own the Garden now and can do what we want with it. Lilith bequeathed it to us," Xavier stated.

Oberon's face turned four shades of red. "Guards, seize them!"

Xavier and I both activated our fire shields and stood on either side of Gwynevere and Praeziel.

The guards retreated from us. Fire glowed around us. Xavier's eyes were a shade of golden amber, and I could only imagine mine were the same.

"We came to you peacefully and would like to leave peacefully. You have no quarrel with Alpha; well, we have no quarrel with you. We can either leave together or we can leave fighting. The choice is yours!" Xavier shouted. "We are the Shining Ones. We are older than you no matter how long ago we were born. You granted us life. You granted us protection. You cannot break your oath!"

"Enough!" Queen Titania shouted. "Stand down," she yelled at the guards. "I have seen and heard enough. We will stand alongside you against Alpha."

"But dear," Oberon began.

"That is final," she hissed at him.

"Thank you, Queen Titania," I replied, bowing. "We shall be on our way."

"Before you go," Queen Titania started. "Gwynevere, dear."

Gwynevere shakily walked up toward the queen. "Yes, ma 'lady," she replied with a curtsy.

"You are welcome back here anytime," she said, smiling. "In fact, all Unseelie from henceforth will be welcome here. It is time we end our own blood feud."

"Thank you, ma' lady," Gwynevere replied, grinning.

We left the castle in merry spirits.

"We did it," I stated. "I can't believe we did it. We have both Seelie and Unseelie courts as an alliance, which means the Watchers and the Nephilim will stand by our side."

"You still have to make good on your promise to Queen Mab," Gwynevere warned.

"Do we have to do it in person?" I asked.

"Yes, you do," the Dark Queen replied.

We all turned in surprise to the sound of her voice.

"Ma' lady," Gwynevere replied, bowing. "We have restored the alliance with the Seelie court, and all Unseelies are once again welcome in front of the nobility. They agreed to fight alongside us for the cause against Alpha. We now own the Garden." She gave the full report and stood back up.

"Excellent news," the Dark Queen replied. She looked at me. "I underestimated all of you. You have our allegiance. You had it from the beginning. Although it would have been a fun game to turn you over to Alpha, we needed you. We can only twist our words to gain what we want, and we did. Do we have your word on the Garden of Eden?" she asked.

"Only if you keep your word about sharing it with all Seelies," I replied.

She snapped her fingers. "Done. It was marvelous meeting both of you. I must, however, return to my realm. You two still have another stop to make. Don't forget about Starfire," the Dark Queen said, winking at Praeziel.

"Thank you, ma' lady," he replied, bowing.

And just like that, she was gone in a flash.

"We should camp here tonight," Praeziel said. "It will be safest right outside the Seelie court realm."

"The last time you said that we were kidnapped," I replied jokingly. "So, since we now have everyone's allegiance, what next?" I asked.

"I must call a Tribunal. We must gather all the Nephilim and prepare them for the uprising against Alpha. It has been long since overdue," Praeziel replied and sighed heavily. "Yea, though I walk through the valley of the shadow of death, I shall fear no evil…"

Sneak Peek of Firefly: The Half-Blood Angel, Book 3 in the Guardians of Light Series

# Chapter One

I HAVE A SECRET. Secrets are something hard to keep. I was a secret that came to light. My mother had an affair with my father, and here I am. However, that's old news. Water under the bridge, so to speak. I never came to know nor love my mother and father. I came to love Alpha as my sole parent. But love is a fickle thing. It can come and go as it pleases, and now, I hold nothing more than loathing and apathy toward Alpha. Whether he knows it to be true is undoubtedly the question. Still, that is not my secret, either. My secret is simple. I am not evil.

I have done horrible things in the name of Alpha. I didn't care. I had no one else to guide me, and I felt that he was guiding me in a way I needed to go. His rhetoric, his law, seemed right and true. I was his little monster, and I enjoyed it. However,

I came to learn he was hiding something from me, something that would change my life forever.

I grew up abnormally because I, myself, was not a typical angel. My mother was special, like her twin soul, and they held powers not seen in any other angel ever created by Alpha and Omega. I had no guidance, and Alpha knew only to use those powers for his own gain. For those differences, I did not age the same as other angels would. I aged expediently into my late teens, where it halted. That was when the more challenging training came, and I found myself forced into training even when I did not want it. Alpha had his reason but never divulged it to me. I found out later. I found out when he swept me away and told me we had to leave the Summit. The Fallen Angels were revolting and reclaiming their places in the purified world he had created. Most believed his actions for requesting someone to oppose him was to create a balance in the world. It was not. He needed to eliminate those who were poisoned and would not follow him to the end with his plans. Those who chose to fall with Omega were the poison, and those left behind were the pure. It was a culling, so to speak. He believed those who remained behind were loyal to him and none other. He was wrong.

There were active members of his angel fleet who were working with those who fell to return them to the Summit. My mother and father were among those angels. Ultimately, in the end, they fell as well to join Omega in her war against Alpha. Even with all of this, I was still Alpha's loyal little soldier. It would be years later that I found out a piece of information that sent my blood to boil. I had siblings that Alpha never told me about.

I had come to learn that I dream, and angels do not dream. At least, typical angels do not. I was far beyond normal. It was within these dreams that I found my siblings. It was always the same place. There was a field in the middle of nowhere with a tree at the center. It was so peaceful and serene. I had been walking these fields for years until, to my surprise, two others joined the place. I hid away from them, envious of their connection. I learned their names while there: Luxina and Xavier. There were times I had nearly come out of my hiding spot to introduce myself to them, to get to know them, but I was cowardly. They hardly knew about each other except in their dreams, and even then, they only knew each other's names. They did not know they were born as twin flames like their mother and father were. So, I sat, and I watched them from afar. I grew fond of them both.

To my horror, Alpha had gained the ability to spy on my dreams along with me. It was then that he became something different. He became distant and malevolent. He locked himself away from me, and it was then I realized I had no one. We had been hiding out in the old Chernobyl buildings, long ago abandoned. I had no idea he was inventing a new race, a new breed of angel. And it was going to start with me.

I traveled with him to the Unseelie Court, where Queen Mab gazed upon me in amazement and desire. She listened to Alpha as he wagered with her, never removing her eyes from me.

"I will give you what you want on two conditions," she replied as Alpha stood by eagerly waiting for her demands. "The first one will be that if you are to succeed, I get to keep this one as my payment," she said, motioning her eyes to me and smiling deviously.

"What is your second condition?" Alpha asked.

Her smile grew wider and even more sinister. "My second condition is if you fail, you yourself will become a prisoner of my court. You may never leave, and you will lose all godly powers you have ever gained. You will, of course, be very well taken care of. However, you pose a threat to all. You have two years to complete the trials."

"That is ludicrous. I would never wager myself for power. You would have to be a fool to strike such a deal," Alpha huffed.

"Well, then you don't get what you came for," Mab replied, holding up a vial of blood. "This is what you wanted, of course, right? A vial of pure blood. My blood?"

Alpha stared at the vile as his face twitched and darkened.

"This could be yours if you are willing to pay the price," she said, twisting the vile back and forth, almost as if she were enchanting Alpha.

"You have no authority over me," Alpha stated. "What makes you think I wouldn't destroy you here and now for the endless amount of blood to gain from your dripping carcass!"

"You cannot harm me," she replied, raising an eyebrow and grinning. "I am older than you and was made by gods that ensured I could never be harmed by gods lower on the spectrum than what they were. Try all you might, you will die before ever touching a hair on my head."

Alpha gulped. I had silently stood by, watching the two of them bicker back and forth. Free of Alpha sounded like a blessing. If he failed, I would be free of his tyranny. Free.

The Dark Queen glanced in my direction as if I had spoken it aloud. I looked around in terror, hoping Alpha had not heard either.

*Do not fear, my little Shining One. He cannot hear you as I can.*

I was a bit fearful and shocked. I looked at Alpha, who was lost in thought while making his decision.

*I can hear you, too?* I asked.

*Of course, young Damian. You have special gifts like your mother, your brother, and your sister. You have an enchantment that needs finished sealing, however. You need to escape Alpha and find your brother and sister and join them on their quest. Together, all three of you will be able to save the world,* she replied.

*What quest? They haven't even met yet,* I replied.

*All in due time, young one.*

"My patience is growing thin, Alpha," Mab seethed. "What shall it be?"

Alpha spoke finally. "I will agree to your conditions."

The Dark Queen laughed maniacally, turned over an hourglass, and looked back at Alpha. "Tick tock, Alpha."

Since that meeting, I have been tortured with various injections. The Dark Queen did not tell him it would be harder for my blood to adhere to the magic since I was not wholly a Shining One. And there were dangers if it did succeed. I may become something completely evil like those vile creatures he had created in the beginning. I didn't want that. But I had no one to stop him from trying them on me.

I lay in agony for days after the first series of injections he created. Hell wasn't even a description that could bring the pain I felt justice. My body rejected injection after injection. With each injection, he would lock himself away, trying to perfect the serum using as little of Queen Mab's blood as he could. He synthesized it to make it last longer. I came to learn that I was not the only one he was using them on as well. He had been taking lower demons created by the Forsaken and experimenting with them as well. They were once humans with just a trace of angelic blood in their systems. Many died at the hands of Alpha. But he didn't care. He wanted this, and whatever Alpha wanted, Alpha received.

I never wanted to be a test dummy. They had to drag me, kicking and screaming, to the chamber to be administered the injections. I fought with everything I had. I froze some of those who dragged me away with my freezing ability. I fought many off in sword combat, killing many of them. I was always outnumbered and always subdued. After so many times of trying to fight, my spirit broke. I eventually began to allow them to lead me to the testing chamber. They would shackle me to a bed while I endured the burning lava injections. Quite a few times, I came close to death, and I begged for mercy to feel the cooling feeling of the abyss envelop me and carry me off to the angel's potter's field. I always recovered at the last minute and would cry for days after wondering what I had done to deserve everything I endured.

The only thing that kept me going and kept me fighting to survive was Luxina and Xavier. I had to keep them from Alpha's grips, even if it meant I was subject to his torturous methods. I knew one day we would be able to meet and greet. I could get to know the family I never had growing up. And I would kill anyone that tried to hurt them.

My only solace and escape were my dreams, where I got to see them. If I could see them, I knew they were safe. They had yet to meet as well and only graced each other in their dreams. The first time I saw them, the power they emitted upon touching each other's hand was monumental. I envied their connection, but I was not jealous of them. They were perfect together. Alpha, at one point, wanted me to do what he had done with Sophie and Incaendiel for all of those years. He wanted me to get Luxina to try and love me, severing her connection with Xavier and becoming less powerful. That's where the twin flames gain their strength, with the connection with their twin soul. I would never do that. I could never do that. However, everyone thinks I am an evil little sentinel for Alpha. If it keeps everyone else I love safe from Alpha, I will let them think that until the day I die.

I remember the day that Lucifer finally made it to Alpha. He didn't even fight his way here. He found one of the sentinels of the Forsaken and bartered his way here, promising Alpha Luxina and Xavier in exchange for me. I immediately hated him. I stood by Alpha's side and glared at him with all of the hate in the world as he proposed to bring Xavier first and then Luxina for Alpha's disposal. All the while, Alpha listened, never intending to let him have me in return. I tried to stop them. I disguised myself and tried to interfere before it was too late. I pretended to be one of the hunting pack that looked for me days on end. That's when I met my mother. I may not think of her much as a mother because I wasn't raised by her, but I could see the good in her heart and the love she had for me.

There were times I would go back to the Summit with them and would watch how she interacted with Xavier, and it made me hate myself. She sacrificed the love for her one son to find the one that was hopeless. Xavier suffered at my expense. Whenever I would catch Sophie alone, we would talk about how much she adored Xavier and also how much he despised her. He felt abandoned by her in her pursuit of finding me. It was I who convinced her to stop searching and return to the Summit to be with Xavier. She needed to protect him from Lucifer because the plan was drawing to a close. If I had acted sooner than later in convincing her to go back and give up, he would not have been harmed by Alpha. There would have been ample time to hide him away. The day came for Lucifer to steal Xavier away, and there wasn't anything I could do to save him without exploiting myself.

I watched as he put our mother in the tower like Alpha had done so many times. It was the same tower I had been born in that he and Sophie were held prisoner in. I already had plans on breaking them out long before Luxina arrived in Chernobyl. What I wasn't expecting was them to dose me along with the others. It made me weak and vulnerable. I had to listen to what I was told without exception. The mind control substance he gave me bent me in ways I couldn't escape until it wore off. I met Xavier long before Luxina arrived, and he already had a steady hate for me. Why wouldn't he hate me? I was the reason he grew up without a mother. She was always looking for me instead of being by his side. I would hate me, too. Our first encounter was less than astounding and not at all what I had imagined meeting my brother for the first time. His pure hatred for me made me falter each time I was in his presence. At times, the injections broke me, and I found myself at his throat, trying to kill him as he egged me on with his venomous words. There would be no doubt that if given the chance to kill me, he would try with all of his might. He had no compassion, just as I didn't. Again, something that can be laid to rest on my shoulders.

When Lucifer came to Alpha ready to go in for Luxina, I wanted to head the party that brought her in. I wanted to keep her as safe as possible. Alpha agreed to let me go, but not before another one of his cocktail injections. I remember slapping her at some point and felt terrible after the injection began to taper off. She was held for a few days before Alpha brought her to his office to meet with her. I expected her to hate me, but I could feel the sorrow and compassion leech from her to me. She wanted to save me. She wanted to truly save me and everyone from the clutches of Alpha. I remember how her heart sank as we walked through the halls, and she heard the cries of the creatures Alpha had been running experiments on. He would inject them, morph them, take their blood after it mutated, and then kill them if they weren't of any use to him.

I witnessed her defiance in front of Alpha when he asked her to join his side. I had heard so many stories of Incaendiel when it came to Alpha, and it was one of the few moments I was glad she had her father's temper and spirit. She would need it to survive the injection. The ones he gave me were vastly different than the ones he had planned to use on her. Even the ones Xavier was subjected to were different than the ones she had. She was receiving almost pure blood from Mab and a cocktail mix of all of the mutt creations he had made.

I watched the moment she struck a nerve in him, and at the last minute, he added an injection that I was unaware of what the contents were. That was until he injected her with them all. He had created an injection that he called Heavenly Hellfire. He gave it to those who refused to cooperate with him. It must have been one of the injections he gave me in the beginning but twice the dose. He could bend the mind to his will through the injections. He wasn't counting on her defiance being even stronger than the injections.

When the Heavenly Hellfire failed, he gave her a series of injections to kill her. Her will to live was just as strong as her defiance. I watched her writhe in agony, and they just kept the injections coming. When I tried to help, when I tried to stave them off from injecting any more of the serum into her, they caught me in the neck with one. It burned through my body, searing every nerve ending I had. I reached out to Xavier with my mind before they pulled me out of the room.

*Get her to Stygia. Find Sophia. Quick, before she dies. She will be the only one to end this war, and Alpha's reign of terror will come to an end. I will find you, and we will stop him together.*

A flicker of acknowledgement rolled across Xavier's face, and I watched through the window of the closing door behind me as he broke the chains free from the wall and swooped her from the place to safety. I, however, was unable to escape to help them. Instead, I was subjected to beatings and torture. I had injections over and over until my body had gone numb and my soul had gone limp. There was hardly any fight left in me. All I could do was think over and over that Xavier had made it to Stygia in time to save Luxina.

I sent him to Sophia for a very specific reason. She knew what to tell them. She knew what to explain to them about what we were. I had come across her once before, and we began to meet in private. She had a plan to help thwart Alpha, but it wouldn't work unless all of the Shining Ones were together. She herself had been to see Mab and knew more things than I could imagine about what we were. We were more than just meager angels. We were almost gods, and together, we were more powerful than Alpha.

It had been several days after Xavier and Luxina had escaped that Alpha came to me in the dungeon. I was chained to the ceiling, suspended off the ground to where my tip toes just barely grazed the floor. He watched me as I spat blood from my mouth. I had just recently been tossed around the room, and my wounds were still fresh.

"You disappointed me, son." His words fell flat as he pulled a chair up and sat down in it. "You helped them escape, and I know you did. What I don't know is how? And most importantly, why?

Why is my best soldier turning against me? I raised you. I gave you everything you could ever want. And this is how you repay me. You throw it back in my face!"

He composed himself and watched for my reaction. I gave him absolutely nothing.

"I have half a mind to feed you to those mutts starving in the cell across from you, but I need you, unfortunately. You have one more chance to prove yourself worthy of me. You will be going along with Lucifer and me to Stygia to get your siblings back. I need all of you together. Are you going to follow my wishes, or are you going just to hang here until your body gives out?" he asked.

I quickly ran everything through my mind. I had to go along. I had to help them escape before he could recapture them. There was no choice.

"I will go with you," I replied.

"Excuse me?" he asked indignantly.

"I will go with you, *father*," I replied once more, emphasizing father for him.

He looked pleased with himself and made a motion with his two forefingers. Asmodeus emerged from the shadows and walked toward me. He released a lever from the wall, and my chain came bounding down from the ceiling. My legs were so weak that I hit the ground with a thud. I could barely feel any of the muscles in my body.

Asmodeus walked over and unshackled by bound wrists.

*You need to run as soon as you can. Alpha will kill you if this plan falls through,* he thought.

I had no idea he knew I could read his thoughts, or anyone knew for that matter. I acknowledged him with my eyes as Alpha watched us. He pulled the chains from around me that had landed in a heap on my legs. I shakily stood stretching out my still numb limbs.

"Mark my words, boy. You fail me and do not kill who I tell you to kill... Well, you can imagine the rest," Alpha stated, turning on his heels, and left the dungeon room with Asmodeus close behind. "We leave at dawn."

I spent all night trying to devise a plan for Xavier and Luxina to escape safely. I hated the thought of having to kill others to protect them, but I have to act like I am on Alpha's side, or else they won't have anyone to help them any longer. I cleaned up all of my cuts and applied a poultice to my bruises when I was back in my room. I winced with each touch as the cuts burned with the herbs.

My door opened, and I thought it was probably Lucifer coming to check on me. However, it was not Lucifer. It was the last person I ever thought I would see walk through that door. It was my mother, Sophie. She ran to my side and threw her arms around me.

"My boy, my sweet, precious boy," she murmured through silent tears of joy.

I winced with pain as she squeezed my broken ribs.

"What have they done to you?" she asked, looking me over and fretting.

She picked up the salve I had been applying and began to gingerly treat my wounds as I stood there in both shock and disbelief. Her fingers worked nimbly over each of the wounds I had until they reached my face. She stopped short and just stared into my eyes as I stared back.

"What are you doing here?" I asked, still confused as to what I was seeing.

She set the jar of salve down on the table, pulled a chair out, and sat down, clasping her hands while leaning forward.

"Alpha attacked the Glade, where a fleet of angels were set up planning an attack to get Luxina and Xavier back," she began. "Before the mountain fully fell, I was grabbed and whisked away to here by Lucifer. He told me he had you three here together all safe."

"Why haven't I seen you before today then?" I asked, stretching a shirt over my head.

"I wanted to see all of you. I wanted to rescue all of you. However, I was chained in a room until I could prove that I wasn't here to stop Alpha. I agreed that it would be safer for all three of you to stay with Alpha than risk trying to take you from here without any help," she explained.

"So, you stood by while they gave Luxina injections? How long has it been since you have been here? Were you here when Xavier was receiving his injections as well? Why didn't you stop them?!" I seethed.

"I was not here for the injections Xavier received. And I was receiving them myself when Luxina arrived," she replied softly. "When Luxina failed to bow to Alpha during his head games, he doubled my doses of Heavenly Hellfire. I made a connection with Luxina and may have said things that were... not truthful to her. I blamed her for my current predicament. The child I had yet to meet, and I was cursing her for defying the one person we all defied after the fall."

Sophie looked away, ashamed.

"I could hear Incaendiel calling out her name to pull her out of that nightmarish place we were stuck together in," she said as she began to weep again. "I said horrible things to him as well prior to the Glade coming down. I'm not even sure if anyone knows I am alive."

I ran my hand through my hair, frustrated.

"Why are you here?" I asked again heatedly.

"I just told you—"

"No, why are you in my room?" I yelled. "Did you think you could come in here and just sweet-talk your way into me calling you mother and collapsing in your arms in tears because you had finally saved me from the evil monster I have called father since I was little?"

She looked a bit stunned at my choice of words.

"My brother and sister are being hunted down like wild animals, and you're sitting here playing tea party with Alpha instead of helping them. You're a terrible excuse for a mother, and you are no mother to me. Please, leave my room," I ordered, pointing in the direction of the door.

"But, I thought," she began, confused. "You don't want to be taken from Alpha?" she asked.

"Not at the risk of my brother and sister falling into his clutches again. They are more important than me. What kind of brother would I be to allow them back here to be tortured more by that devil in disguise? I would be no better than you or Lucifer."

I stared at her long and hard.

"Lucifer," she started when I cut her off again.

"Don't get me started about that pathetic waste of space. You're honestly going to sit there and defend him when he was the one that orchestrated the entire kidnapping plot of both of your children. I am not more important than two lives." I held my door open for her to leave. I looked her dead in the eyes and said, "You will never be my mother, and Lucifer will never be my father. I don't have a family. Had it been my decision, you would have died in that mountain."

Dumbfounded, she just gave me a nod and left the room. I slammed the door closed behind her and threw myself backward on my bed, landing on my back. I would never understand her rhetoric of thinking. Had she been totally brainwashed? I stared at the ceiling for quite some time before another knock came on my door.

"For the love of all that is holy," I muttered, standing to answer the knock.

I opened the door, and yet another face I despised stood before me. Lilith, Omega, whatever you want to call her, loomed in the doorway before letting herself in the room. She walked around the room, lifting things up and setting them back down. I watched her, completely unaware of what she was trying to accomplish. She unscrewed the lightbulb in the room, and once she was satisfied with whatever search she was doing, she sat down in the chair my mother had just left not too long ago.

"Hello, Damian. We have yet to formally meet," she stated after a moment of silence.

"I'm Damian. You're Lilith. We have met now, so you can leave," I replied hastily, motioning to the door.

She studied me with eyes that were unfamiliar. A glimmer of life floated through her eyes before they glazed back over. She swallowed, slightly clearing her throat before she spoke to me again.

"When you leave to go with Alpha on this trip, you must escape him once Xavier and Luxina are safe," she declared, unwavering in her lack of emotion.

"I already know. He plans to kill me if his plan fails," I replied, annoyed.

"You could only wish for death for what he has planned for you after it fails," she whispered.

"I just spent days being strung up by my arms with my feet barely touching the ground to stand up. I'm sure whatever it is, I can handle it," I retorted.

"You have such a fighting spirit. If I didn't know any better, I would swear your father was Incaendiel instead of the lousy one that brought you forth," she remarked, fire blazing in her eyes.

"That is something I can agree with," I replied with a wicked grin. "My father is a piece of crap that deserves nothing more than to be doused in gasoline and dropped into the lake of fire."

"Now, since we are on the same page," she decreed, careening her neck and smiling, "let's get down to the matter at hand. All three of you need to be as far away from Alpha as possible after this raid ends. Unless you can absolutely convince him that you had nothing to do with their escape... "

"I don't know how many times I have to stress to you people that I don't care what Alpha does to me as long as Xavier and Luxina are safe," I barked, exasperated. "I hate repeating myself over and over."

"For the power of the Shining Ones to work, to put an end to Alpha, all three of you have to be together," Lilith urged. "You weren't supposed to have become. I never imagined that Sophie would succumb to weakness in that tower. So, when Luxina and Xavier were born, they were not born with the full power they should have had. You are the missing piece in all of that. You have to make it to them and join them. Or else, all of this will have been for naught."

"If I wasn't supposed to exist, I wouldn't," I snarled. "What makes you so sure it's me that wasn't supposed to exist and not one of them?"

She eyed me, pursing her lips. I could see I struck a nerve. Everyone knew about how my mother had me and what she did. She had betrayed Incaendiel. So, most think I wasn't supposed to exist because of that. Had Sophie never been in the tower with Lucifer, I wouldn't exist here because she would have never been tempted. However, it doesn't say anywhere that twin souls have to be born at the same time, so it is quite possible that I am supposed to be and Xavier not. However, either way, it doesn't change anything. I will protect him either way.

"Why are you helping us when you are joining forces with Alpha?" I asked suspiciously.

"Because out of everything I have made in this world, Sophia and Incaendiel will be the one thing I cherish the most. In extension, you three are also my cherished creations. I will not see my creations destroyed. If it comes down to it, Alpha will have to destroy me in the end and then figure out how to rebuild the universe alone. I have never stopped loving Alpha. He is my other half no matter how screwed up he is. It was inevitable for us to come back together."

"What do you suggest I do then?" I asked.

"What we all have been telling you to. Run."

Kasey Hill has lived in Franklin County, VA, for most of her adult life and is a versatile writer known for her work in several genres, including urban fantasy, horror, thriller, paranormal romance, and metaphysical/New Age topics. She has authored both fiction and non-fiction, with a particular interest in Wicca, specializing in Trinitarian Wicca as the historical archivist with an upcoming historical account of the shift from polytheism to monotheism in Abrahamic religions, where she has published non-fiction works exploring the subject.

Her fiction often dives into the supernatural and the macabre, blending mythological elements with modern storytelling. She has published multiple novels, poetry collections, and short stories. Notable works include her *Guardians of Light* series in the mythology fantasy genre, and her poetry that has received recognition for its depth and emotional resonance. As she grows in the horror genre, she has a particular penchant for Southern Gothic storytelling, such as her Adult Horror novel *Devil's Claw* and her Young Adult horror series, *The Whispering Spirits* featuring *The Haunting at Foxwood Village* and *Dark Coven*. She has several

Horror short stories circulating for anthologies and Ezines featuring her unique style of worldbuilding.

In addition to her writing, Kasey Hill has also contributed to the Wiccan and occult community through her non-fiction work, making her a multi-faceted author with a broad range of interests and expertise.